UNDER A GLASS BELL

Under a Glass Bell

AND OTHER STORIES

 Anaïs Nin

Introduction by Elizabeth Podnieks

Swallow Press
Ohio University Press
Athens, Ohio

Swallow Press
An imprint of Ohio University Press, Athens, Ohio 45701
www.ohioswallow.com

Front cover photograph courtest istockphoto.

Back cover photograph: Anïas Nin at her press, New York, 1940s.

Courtesy Anïas Nin Trust

Cover design by Beth Pratt

Printed in the United States of America
Swallow Press / Ohio University Press books are printed on acid-free paper ⊗ ™

24 23 22 21 20 19 18 17 16 15 14   5 4 3 2 1

Library of Congress Cataloging-in-Publication Data

Nin, Anaïs, 1903–1977.
[Short stories. Selections]
Under a Glass Bell and Other Stories / Anaïs Nin ; Introduction by Elizabeth
Podnieks. — New Swallow Press edition.
    pages cm
Includes bibliographical references.
This new Swallow Press edition restores the original order of the stories from the
1948 edition.
ISBN 978-0-8040-1147-1 (pb : acid-free paper)
I. Podnieks, Elizabeth, [date]– II. Title.
PS3527.I865A6 2013
813'.54—dc23
                    2013038255

Contents

"Sponges of Secret Sorrows"

Introducing the Stories in *Under a Glass Bell*

ELIZABETH PODNIEKS

Building Bridges

"In being deprived of publication I am deprived of existence, forced back into solitude, disconnected from life. Being published would have been a bridge between myself and American life. Without it, it means a shrunken life, a small world, less expansion and contact with the world."[1] So writes Anaïs Nin (1903–1977) in her diary, lamenting her exclusion from the American literary establishment. When she recorded these words in New York in April 1941, she had been a prolific writer of diaries and poetic prose fiction for nearly three decades, yet had little published material to show for it.[2] Her desires to connect with her readers and to become a global presence are two of the most profound forces that drove and shaped her artistic life. Her writing was predicated on her need to build bridges, to communicate across and beyond physical, psychological, and literary borders.

Nin was a French American author who lived, wrote, and published in Europe and the United States, and thus her identity as well as her oeuvre unfolded within a transatlantic context. She was born in Neuilly-sur-Seine, a suburb of Paris, in 1903, to Spanish Cuban parents of multinational backgrounds who had met and married in Havana. Her mother, Rosa Culmell, of Danish and French descent, was a concert singer; her father, Joaquín Nin y Castellanos, of Spanish and Cuban descent, was a concert pianist. When Nin was ten years old, her father abandoned the family for his mistress, advising his wife to take Anaïs and her brothers, Joaquín and Thorvald, to live with his parents in Barcelona. From there they sailed to New York to join Culmell's relatives.

Traveling away from her father in July 1914, Nin began her now-(in)famous diary as an extended letter to him. She describes this early diary as "The bridge. It was my first bridge. To reach my father. To reach Europe" (3:115). Nin spent the next decade in New York, growing up determined to be a writer. She married banker Hugh (Hugo) Guiler in 1923, and when he received a promotion in December 1924, the couple, along with Nin's mother and brothers, relocated to Paris. Nin honed her literary skills over the next fifteen years, filling dozens of diary volumes while concurrently transforming some of her autobiography into fiction. With the onset of war, the family was forced out of France in September 1939 and returned to New York where, as we heard from Nin above, she grew increasingly frustrated by her inability to secure commercial publishing contracts and gain public recognition.

Desperate to claim a space in literary history, she decided to publish her own books. To that end, in December 1941, with her lover Gonzalo Moré, she purchased a secondhand printing press that "operated like an old-fashioned sewing machine, by a foot pedal" (3:179), and in January 1942 had it installed in an attic studio at 144 MacDougal Street in Greenwich Village. Nin named her new firm the Gemor Press for Moré, and the pair set to work typesetting by hand and printing Nin's manuscripts. In 1942, they brought out *Winter of Artifice*, consisting of two novellas. Then, in February 1944, they released her collection of short stories, *Under a Glass Bell*, which proved to be the literary event for which she had been longing.

The printing was completed on February 16, 1944, and the book launched on February 24 at the Wakefield Gallery, where Guiler's copper engravings were being exhibited. Under the pseudonym of Ian Hugo, Nin's banker husband had turned to art and filmmaking as a sideline career, and he had crafted the cover and seventeen illustrations for this first edition of the stories.[3] Nin reports on the book's impressive debut: "I am receiving my due! Affection, response, feelings to answer my feelings. Sincere success, no falseness."[4] The book was sold primarily at the iconic midtown Gotham Book Mart (in business from 1920 to 2007), part store and part literary salon operated by owner Frances Steloff, Nin's friend. Not only did the first three hundred copies sell out in less than three weeks, but the book was positively reviewed by the preeminent critic Edmund Wilson in the April 1, 1944, issue of the *New Yorker*. Nin's biographer Deirdre Bair contends that this review, discussed in more detail below, "did more than all others to establish Anaïs Nin as a serious writer of some importance. . . . It was every writer's dream review" (297). As Nin revels in her accomplishment, "The connection I made with a few people from the publication of *Under a Glass Bell* seemed like the breaking of a shell (how many shells?), a second birth (how many births?), a becoming visible and tangible" (3:312).

Nin's much-anticipated exposure resulted in her first commer-cial contract, with E. P. Dutton signing on in December 1945 to publish her fiction, including *Ladders to Fire* (1946), *Children of the Albatross* (1947), and the expanded *Under a Glass Bell and Other Stories* (1948). Almost sixty years later, with the reissuing of this present edition from Swallow Press/Ohio University Press, Nin can enjoy yet another "birth" and "a becoming visible and tangible" to new audiences.

✤ ✤ ✤ ✤

Although Nin went on to publish many works of fiction over the next two decades, she is known today primarily as the author of some of the most sustained and sensational diaries of the twentieth century. Spanning the years 1914 to 1974, from her childhood to a few years before her death, the diaries were published during her lifetime and then posthumously in sixteen volumes between 1966 and 2013. Despite her prolific output and ongoing cultural presence, Nin has entered posterity, according to Bair, "as a minor writer." However, Bair qualifies, "I insist upon one distinction: that she must be judged a *major* minor writer" (xviii). Nin's work emerged out of and contributed to the period known as modernism, a term encompassing radical cultural, aesthetic, and political movements taking shape around the Western world between roughly 1890 and

1945. Writers, artists, and musicians responded to the Industrial Revolution and the consequent modernization, urbanization, and commercialization of society in the late nineteenth and early twentieth centuries by experimenting with style and content that broke from Victorian forms and conventions. While modernism has been gendered male and masculine in canonical literary history, from the 1980s on scholars have been revising this history from feminist perspectives and privileging the roles of women.[5]

Bair contends that Nin "consistently discerned what was worthwhile in the literature and culture of her time. She was a shining exemplar of the modernist dictum 'Make it new,' for she was prescient enough to poise herself directly in the path of all that was fresh, exciting, and frequently controversial." Bair further asserts that "the twentieth century will be remembered for many concepts that brought sweeping societal change, and Anaïs Nin was among the pioneers who explored three of the most important: sex, the self, and psychoanalysis. When future generations seek to understand how these evolved in our time, Anaïs Nin will be the major minor writer whose work they must consult" (xviii). My aim in this introduction is to point to what present-day readers will discover in *Under a Glass Bell* and to suggest the ongoing value and relevance of the stories to a twenty-first-century generation.

Nin's production of a lifelong journal had a direct impact on her short stories and novels. In *The Novel of the Future*, her 1968 treatise on modern fiction, Nin tells us: "I may say that it was my experience as a novelist which enabled me to edit *The Diary* at all" (153–54). In like manner, we may say that it was her experience as a diarist that enabled her to conceive of the stories in the first place, for each one is drawn from her journal entries, at times in nearly identical prose. She muses in the *Novel* passage above: "Here the conflict lies in the usefulness of the diary as biographical source, as against the desire of the publisher and the reader to 'get on with the story'" (154). While it is certainly feasible to approach *Under a Glass Bell* with no background knowledge and simply "get on with the story," readers equipped with autobiographical details will appreciate that Nin's entire aesthetic agenda was shaped by the conflation of life and art, fact and imagination.

Nin explains that "both diary and fiction tended towards the same goal: intimacy with people, with experience, with life itself" (155) and that "in the diary the preoccupation with the art of expression began more and more to work in harmony with the fiction" (158). Ultimately, she claims, "Without the diary, the prose poem, and fiction I could not have achieved the *relation* between them. It is the *relation* which interested me, the *connection*, the *bridges*, the *interaction*, the *dynamics of relation* among human beings as well as among the ways of expression human beings use" (161). Acknowledging the symbiotic nature of her texts, I turn to "the usefulness of the diary as biographical source" to assist in identifying the real-life personages, places, and events depicted in *Under a Glass Bell*.

Textual Contexts

The stories are drawn directly from diary entries made between 1933 and 1946, with the exception of "The Labyrinth," which invokes Nin's first diary of July to August 1914. Ten of the thirteen stories unfold in Paris; two are set in New York, and one in Morocco. The first story, "Houseboat," takes place on *La Belle Aurore*, which Nin rented from February to August 1938, on the Quai du Pont Royal on the banks of the Seine in Paris. The story likely also draws on her time in late 1936 and early 1937 aboard her first rented boat, *Nanankepichu*. Ostensibly a work studio, the boats were used by Nin for her liaisons with Moré. The second story, "The Mouse," features a woman referred to in the diary as Albertine and "the Mouse" who worked as the maid on the houseboat. In the titular piece, "Under a Glass Bell," protagonist Jeanne is Louise de Vilmorin (1902–1969)—Nin gave her the pseudonym "Jeanne" in her diary as well—a French writer and journalist, married to real-estate mogul Henry Leigh Hunt, whose banker was Nin's husband.

The next two stories focus on male figures: "The Mohican" is the French astrologer Conrad Moricand (1887–1954); "*Je suis le plus malade des Surréalistes*" refers to Antonin Artaud (1896–1948), French surrealist actor, playwright, and founder of the Theater of Cruelty. "Ragtime" recalls an August 1936 outing Nin made with

Moré to the ragpickers' village on the outskirts of Paris. "The Labyrinth" reenvisions Nin as an eleven-year-old in a setting that corresponds to her maternal aunt's home in Queens, New York, where Nin first stayed upon her emigration in 1914. This story is followed by "Through the Streets of My Own Labyrinth," based on her April 1936 vacation in Fez, Morocco.

Nin then turns to artists in Paris in "The All-Seeing," which deals with French painter Albert Jean Grand-Carteret (1903–1954), and "The Eye's Journey," about German painter Hans Reichel (1892–1958). "The Child Born Out of the Fog" depicts the relationship between "Nancy Banks, a lovely blonde girl who is married to Don, a Negro guitar player," whom Nin met in New York in April 1946 (4:135); it is also based on her meeting with African American author Richard Wright and his family (4:145). "Hejda" traces the emigration to Paris of a Persian woman named in the diary only as "Moira," a pseudonym. Lastly, "Birth" describes the August 1934 termination of Nin's pregnancy in Paris during her long-term affair with writer Henry Miller. In "Birth" and the first volume of *The Diary*, Nin presents the event as a tragic stillbirth; in the unexpurgated volume *Incest*, she treats the same subject matter but reveals that in fact she had an abortion.

✤ ✤ ✤ ✤

The order of the stories as described here is according to their arrangement in this 2014 edition. This sequence is the one designed by Nin herself for the 1948 Dutton edition and the one that would "remain uniform for almost 50 years" (460), as noted by scholar Benjamin Franklin V; once she had established her thirteen-story order, "she never changed it, despite opportunities for restructuring" (472). In 1995, Swallow Press/Ohio University Press issued a new edition, edited by Nin's agent, Gunther Stuhlmann, who rearranged the stories, retaining the original position of only two. In his foreword Stuhlmann justifies this decision as seeking "to reflect, to some extent, the sequence of events and persons recorded in the diary which served as their inspiration rather than the uncertain chronological order in which they were written or published." Franklin, however, shows that only four of the thirteen stories in Stuhlmann's version actually adhere to this "sequence of events," leading Franklin to urge Swallow Press/Ohio University Press to "republish *Under a Glass Bell* with the stories arranged according to Nin's wishes" (477). Franklin, convinced that Nin followed "a compelling literary logic" in structuring the book (461), is perhaps bolstered by Nin, who states in *The Novel of the Future*: "Spontaneity belongs in the first jet of writing, but some disciplined selectivity and cutting should follow in editing. While I have enjoyed the informality of the diary writing, I also enjoyed compressing and cutting the short stories in *Under a Glass Bell* until they were gemlike. I would not change one word today, twenty years later" (85). We might easily extend her sentiments to suggest that she "would not change" the *order* of one story, either. With no substantive evidence to favor Stuhlmann's structure, I believe that Swallow Press/Ohio University Press's decision to restore Nin's original artistic vision for her work is appropriate and underscores an obvious rationale for this new edition.

Franklin's observation of Nin's "compelling literary logic" helps us make sense of the stories, which are written in an often challenging poetic prose style informed by surrealism, a major aesthetic and political branch of modernism. As defined by *The Oxford Dictionary of Literary Terms*, surrealism is "an anti-rational movement of imaginative liberation in European (mainly French and Spanish) art and literature in the 1920s and 1930s, launched by André Breton in his *Manifeste du Surréalisme* (1924)." Influenced in part by Sigmund Freud's valuing of the unconscious and by late-nineteenth-century French symbolist poets who relied on evocative imagery to express private moods and sentiments, surrealists attempt to "break down the boundaries between rationality and irrationality, exploring the resources and revolutionary energies of dreams, hallucinations, and sexual desire." In *The Novel of the Future* Nin identifies with this movement: "In Paris, in the thirties, many writers around me were breaking the molds of the conventional novel and experimentation was encouraged. More than that, French literature at that time was dedicated to war against the cliché, the obvious, the traditional, and the conventional—all energies were engaged in innovation"—as was Nin, who "felt part of a pioneering group" (1). Having early on adopted Carl Jung's credo "Proceed from the dream outward," Nin explains: "The definition of a dream is: ideas and images in the mind *not under the command of reason*. It is not necessarily an image or an idea that we have during sleep. It is merely an idea or image which escapes the control of reasoning or logical or rational mind." "Most fiction writers," she specifies, "use dreams decoratively, without re-lating them to daily life, but the contemporary writer is becoming more expert at detecting the influence of one upon the other" (5–6).

It is this "expert" fusion that Edmund Wilson recognized in *Under a Glass Bell* when he reviewed the book for the *New Yorker* in 1944. Nin copied his review into her diary, which I quote here: "The pieces in this collection belong to a peculiar genre sometimes cultivated by the late Virginia Woolf. They are half short stories, half dreams, and they mix a sometimes exquisite poetry with a homely realistic observation." Wilson goes on: "There are passages in her prose which may suffer a little from an hallucinatory vein of writing which the Surrealists have overdone: a mere reeling-out of images, each of which is designed to be surprising but which strung together, simply fatigue. In Miss Nin's case, however, the imagery does convey something and is always appropriate. . . . Half woman, half childlike spirit, she shops, employs servants, wears dresses, suffers the pains of childbirth, yet is likely at any moment to be volatilized into a superterrestrial being who feels things that we cannot feel." He ends by affirming that "the main thing to say is that Miss Nin is a very good artist, as perhaps none of the literary Surrealists is" (3:310–11). Wilson catapulted Nin from obscurity to the *New Yorker*–hued limelight of the literary establishment, but the glow soon dimmed; upon the commercial publication in 1948 she tersely summarizes: "Clippings and reviews of *Under a Glass Bell*. Not one line of under-standing" (5:25).

Typesetting the book in January 1944, Nin felt "joy at achieve-ment and certainty that the stories are poetically valuable" (3:303). Alan Swallow, who became Nin's American publisher in the 1960s, was eager to keep the collection in print since it remained her "most popular book" (Bair, 450). And in that same decade, Nin told scholar

Oliver Evans: "If I had to choose one book by which I would like to be remembered, it is this one"—*Under a Glass Bell* (quoted in Cushman, 110). To date, however, there remains a dearth of criticism on the text. Keith Cushman reiterates in 1978 Nin's reproach to her reviewers—"Not one line of understanding"—when he argues that "even today" Nin's "intention has never been fully grasped by readers of the volume, for no one seems to have observed the special unity of the collection." Commenting that critics have (mis)read the stories as "a gathering of disparate short fictions," he posits that Nin employed "a single shaping and controlling vision": "A recurring series of words, images, and motifs appears throughout the collection, linking stories imagistically and providing continuity and artistic resonance" (110–11).

Franklin similarly believes that the stories "cohere as a unified whole" and suggests they "might beneficially be read as a short-story cycle, or sequence" such that they "flow naturally, one from the other" (462–63). However, his certainty that Nin "organized her collection so it would progress logically . . . from the first story to the last" (464) puts him at odds with Cushman's declaration that the stories are "interchangeable" (111) and lack "external organization" (114). I read *Under a Glass Bell* through their composite approaches, which speak to Nin's modernist experimentation with style and structure: as a short-story sequence that can be tracked in linear fashion from beginning to end and also in circular motion along the way, in both cases testifying to external and internal logics calculated and calibrated by Nin.

Themes and Meanings

The controlling image for the titular story and hence for the collection as a whole is the glass bell, a dome-shaped glass covering used to protect young or weak plants from outside and potentially harmful elements such as frost. Nin adopts the gardening device as metaphor for the rarified, stifling, and suffocating atmosphere engulfing her characters. As Nin describes in the story, "The light from the icicle bushes threw a patina over all objects, and turned them into bouquets of still flowers kept under a glass bell. The glass bell covered the flowers, the chairs, the whole room, the panoplied beds, the statues, the butlers, all the people living in the house. The glass bell covered the entire house." Countless related images and motifs depicting characters trapped in and seeking release from both real and imagined (dreamy, fantastical, hallucinatory) locations and states of being recur throughout the collection, and can be grouped in clusters such as the following: house, asylum, cell, prison, cage, cave, chain, tomb, laboratory; earth, water, lunar space; key, gate, window, bridge; drugs, alcohol, poison, anesthetic; acting, gesture, performance, exhibition; veil, labyrinth, secret, silence; sanity and insanity; winter, ice, fire, light, dark; love, sex, obsession, hunger, drown; cruelty, pain, torture, fever, demon, savage; elite, aristocratic, sophisticated; stagnant, timeless, voyage, metamorphosis, transformation; mirror, eyes, blind, tears, lost, abandoned; birth, life, and death.

Nin explores the modern condition as she experienced and observed it at midcentury. In a prose style combining a concrete rendering of detail with the psychological realism of surrealism, she places her characters in a wasteland that is at once imaginatively universal and historically specific. While a close reading of all the stories is beyond my scope here, I want to address an ongoing charge leveled against Nin, namely what Nancy Scholar calls Nin's "indifference to social and political realities." Scholar believes that "in terms of Nin's relation to the outside world, all her work is 'under a glass bell'" (311–12). The bell produces, I believe, a tension between the contents isolated on the inside and the external forces operating on or against them. In terms of the stories, we can see that this tension is driven by characters who seek escape from, while nonetheless being affected by, their historical situations. It is precisely through making the real world the backdrop to her dream world that Nin demonstrates, contra Scholar, an ongoing awareness of her "social and political realities" and a desire to compensate for and critique them through the realm of art.

The stories were written and revised between 1933 and 1946, that is, in the period leading up to, during, and after both the Spanish Civil War and World War II. Within her diary Nin reflects on the role of the writer to oppose via literary creation these destructive and traumatizing world events. In October 1936, in response to "a rehearsal for war," she feels: "I may be able to escape the fatality of historical time, the tragedies of daily life, the cruelty and destructiveness of the world into poetic life, the eternal" (2:128). In April 1940, while crafting "The All-Seeing," she finds that "the war news is so terrible that it causes a kind of catalepsy. To revive I plunge into writing" (3:32). In the winter of 1942, in conversation with Moira, protagonist of "Hejda," Nin affirms the power of storytelling: "One's courage is renewed. Who spoke of ivory towers? Laboratories of the soul. Where essences are manufactured which defeat ugliness, poverty, debts, humiliations, defeats" (3:235–36). The stories in *Under a Glass Bell* were produced in this laboratory where Nin transmuted some of the unpalatable and untenable realities of her sociopolitical times into art.

The collection establishes its historical context from the beginning, as the narrator of "Houseboat" describes the local tramps who give her "the news of the day, of the approach of war." In "The Mohican," the eponymous astrologer "saw only the madness of the world, the approach of a great world—engulfing catastrophe," and "was now walking through the city merely to warn us of the disruption of Europe." At the conclusion, "when the Germans came, because of his charts, maps, calculations, and predictions of the death of Hitler, he was arrested as a celestial saboteur." The protagonist of "*Je suis le plus malade des Surréalistes*," Pierre, confined to a straitjacket, invokes the Nazis when he informs his doctor that "the black eagles are envious, they are the friends of evil and they are against me. They come, six of them, in gray suits, and they pursue me." And in "The Eye's Journey," painter Hans "always painted a small human eye in the corner" of his pictures; "the small fixed eye in the corner of the painting was hypnotized with terror. A world about to vanish always, on the brink of absolute catastrophe."

The stories also invoke and critique oppressive institutional forces. At the end of "Houseboat," for example, the narrator and the other residents of the river are cast out, sent literally up the Seine to the periphery or margins of the city because the "King of

England was expected for a visit and he would not like the sight of the houseboats." The barges thus passed "into exile." Originally published in 1941 under the title "I Shall Never Forgive the King of England"[6] (George VI), the story can be read as an indictment of imperialist power. The medical establishment is also exposed as cold, hostile, and inhumane in several stories. Suffering from an infection following an abortion, the unmarried protagonist of "The Mouse" is essentially left to bleed to death in a hospital waiting room. In "*Je suis*," Pierre is committed to a mental asylum where he endures physical and psychological abuse by the medical personnel, as does Hans, isolated in a "cell" in "The Eye's Journey." And in "Birth," as the narrator is strapped down and tries to deliver her stillborn child, nurses humiliate her while the doctor, angry and impatient, threatens her with his sharp instruments. Relatedly, the eponymous Hejda is "bound" and "oppressed" by the patriarchal control of her husband, Molnar. These stories present vulnerable subjects as prisoners whose bodies and psyches are subjected to authorized, state-sanctioned restrictions and tortures.

Nin's treatment of political and personal power can be considered in terms of international and transnational themes associated with modernism. Douglas Mao and Rebecca L. Walkowitz chart the field of "the new modernist studies" emerging from the 1999 creation of the Modernist Studies Association (MSA) and subsequent journals and conferences dedicated to modernism. Tracing multiple currents that represent the "expansion" of modernist scholarship to date, they identify "transnational exchange" as a particularly salient strand (738). Defined by Merriam-Webster as "extending or going beyond national boundaries," transnationalism takes its cue from modernism as produced out of and reflecting international circumstances and identities. International modernism can refer to writers themselves as well as to their fictional characters who are in states of voluntary or involuntary exile from their geographic homelands, and who have emigrated to or inhabit urban centers of modernism such as London, Paris, and Berlin, for instance. Whereas international modernism privileges specifically Anglo-American contexts, the transnational turn encourages scholarship in more global terms. Transnational perspectives also direct

attention to figures who are alien, marginalized, and powerless, func-
tioning outside the realm of mainstream, conservative cultures.

Nin's characters embody identities of difference in multiple ways.
Exposed, as we have seen, to institutional forces threatening their safety
and autonomy, characters take comfort in but are concurrently debili-
tated by their illicit habits and passions. Tramps ("Houseboat"), Hans
("The Eye's Journey"), and the mother of Jeanne ("Under a Glass
Bell") are alcoholics; Pierre ("*Je suis*") and Jean ("The All-Seeing")
are drug addicts. Condemned to a present in which the future is terrifying and uncertain, and in which human relations seem increasingly
artificial and inauthentic, characters like Jeanne, Jean, Pierre, Hejda,
and the Mohican have become actors, exhibitionists, and stripteasers
who wear costumes, perform only with gestures, and play roles. At
once revealing and concealing their disparate selfhoods, they are unable to achieve genuine human connections. The stories further offer
a vision of relationships on the borders of legitimacy, revealing that in
the modern world love in its many forms is elusive, taboo, destructive,
or dangerous, in any combination. The "Houseboat" narrator can
only "await the phantom lover" who forbids her "each time to love";
Jeanne is driven mad by her incestuous relationship with her brothers; "Mouse" gets pregnant out of wedlock; the protagonist in "Birth"
graphically delivers a stillborn child; the Mohican has homosexual encounters with a Turkish boy; and Sarah and Don are persecuted as an
interracial couple ("The Child Born Out of the Fog").

The stories represent a wide spectrum of class and cultural posi-
tions. Reflecting the democratizing impulses of modernism to regard
any subject as worthy of literary treatment, Nin peoples her stories
with a motley assortment of characters including aristocrats, artists,
addicts, bohemians, hoboes, ragpickers, and servants. These disparate folk inhabit the wasteland of their physical and psychic wounds
and unconventional behaviors, a universe in which dreams become
nightmares, and in which they feel fragmented, afraid, and often dead
in life. Existing on geographic and symbolic margins, they pass, like
the houseboat, into some form of "exile." "Houseboat" is the perfect
vessel for Nin to launch her other stories, setting up this overarching
theme of being displaced or dispossessed as a central condition in

her contemporary world. The narrator, like the tramps around her boat, "had fallen out of the crowd life" and "walked and slept in counter-rhythm to the world." Such displacement, however, affords new opportunities and experiences, as she reports that the key to the boat is "the key to the little door to my life in the infinite"; "Every time I inserted the key in the lock, I felt this snapping of cords, this lifting of anchor, this fever of departure. Once inside the houseboat, all the voyages began," reminding us of the power of stories to pro-vide a means to escape one's stultifying or repressive environs, as we heard Nin note earlier.

All the characters embark on physical and psychological voyages to destinations that may be familiar and foreign, exterior and interior. Stories map space and place in often national terms, as they are set in or feature characters from France, Germany, Roumania, Morocco, Persia, Peru, and New York. Characters define themselves or are de-fined by others according to racial identity, evidenced for instance by the Mohican who "believed himself the last of the Mohicans, a faded, high-cheeked Indian transplanted from lost continents," or Hejda, who "at seventeen . . . left the Orient and the veils, but . . . retained an air of being veiled" as she tries to negotiate her Arabian heri-tage with her desire to be a liberated artist in Paris. As a black man and a white woman, Don and Sarah fear racially motivated attack in "The Child Born Out of the Fog," especially with the birth of their daughter, Pony: "stones were thrown at them, and Don's life was in danger"; "so they never walked together and [Sarah] could not carry Pony safely through the streets" of New York. Stories such as these illuminate the inflection of transnational themes within the collection and the impact of nationhood and race on the experiences of the characters.

Webs of Connection

Mao and Walkowitz assert that a feature of the transnational turn is scholarship that "argues for the centrality of transnational cir-culation and translation in the production of modernist art" (739). This notion connects with their discussion of "Media in an Age of

Mass Persuasion," where they outline the "marketing of modernism" as one of the most significant topics to have emerged in modernist studies over the past decade, one that resonates fully with Nin as a self-publisher, promoter, and distributor of her own texts. The new modernist studies acknowledge as inescapable the relationship between high (modernist, elite) and low (commodity, mass culture) art, and as such relate to "how modernism built its audiences" (744). Nin bought her own press and actively secured an audience for her Gemor edition by initiating a subscription campaign, selling advance copies to friends and local supporters before she began the typesetting. The unique and high-art quality of the limited Gemor edition is manifested in its mode of individual production, as Nin tells her diary: "I live for days with each page. I set each word. I bind each line" (3:303).[7] Nin was aided by her husband, who financed the press, and by her small group of literary friends like Miller and Steloff, who helped publicize and sell the book. The success of the Gemor edition led to her commercial contract with Dutton; like countless modernists Nin worked within and directed her work to both coterie and mass marketplaces.

The transatlantic production of the stories is signaled not only by Nin's Spanish-Cuban-French-American heritage but also by the fact that although most of the stories were written in Paris, they were revised in New York, and typeset with the help of the Peruvian Moré; some were published as individual stories in Europe, Mexico, Cuba, and the United States; and the book has been translated into French, Spanish, Catalan, Italian, German, and Dutch. The collection has been available in a Kindle edition since 2010. As it has shifted in status from a handmade, to a commercial, to a digital edition, the text has extended its reach from local to global audiences. A work of literature and a textual artifact, *Under a Glass Bell* is an exemplary model by which we can expand our understanding of modernism at the intersections of high and low art forms; national, transatlantic, and transnational borders; and the technologies of creation, dissemination, and reproduction.

✤ ✤ ✤ ✤

Virginia Woolf claimed that "fiction is like a spider's web, attached ever so lightly perhaps, but still attached to life at all four corners" (47). This observation plays out in *Under a Glass Bell*, where Nin fuses the real and the surreal, the historic and the imaginary. Thus, for instance, the narrator of "The Labyrinth" "walked pinned to a spider web of fantasies" while Nin herself affirms, during the period of writing the stories, "It seems to me that all my creation is an effort to weave a web of connection with the world" (3:231). The stories showcase connections between the characters through recurring images and motifs, and through shared experiences. The stories further allow us to make connections between the mid-twentieth century in which they were composed and our own twenty-first century, evidenced in transgenerational themes: global war and environmental catastrophe; the marginalizing of individuals marked by difference; the difficulty of forming meaningful relationships in an alienating world; addiction and substance abuse; taboo or alternative sexual behaviors; the intervention of the state and other institutions in our civil liberties; and the use of art to express the spirit of the age.

Almost all the protagonists are artists of some sort, be they painters, musicians, actors, poet-astrologers, or writers, yet they typically fail to find redemption through their creative media. Hoping for transformation, metamorphosis, rebirth, they are instead subjected to persecution, debilitating obsessions, loss (of love, sanity, liberty), and they stagnate or suffer various forms of symbolic or actual death along a narrative continuum. Within the story sequence, we begin with the "Houseboat" narrator who "traveled out of the landscape of despair"; but her vehicle of deliverance winds up incapacitated, holed up at "an old barge surrounded by rotting skeletons of barges." At midpoint in the book, the narrator of "The Labyrinth" encounters "white sponges of secret sorrows set in a lace of plant skeletons" and plant material "flowing together through the river bed of stillborn desires." And the final story of the collection, "Birth," recounts a literal stillbirth and the near-death of a mother. All the stories are "sponges" absorbing the "secret sorrows" of the characters. So, too, is Nin. In January 1939, listening to the news about the Spanish Civil War and pending World War II, she becomes "metamorphosed into a sponge, absorbing all the tears of the world, accumulating sorrows, unable to erase anything" (2:318). Accumulating these sorrows in *Under a Glass Bell*, Nin made art out of her bleak contemporary vision, and used it to "weave a web of connection with the world." "Through the Streets of My Own Labyrinth" concludes with the diary-writing narrator walking through Fez: "The little donkey—my diary burdened with my past—with small faltering steps is walking to the market." *Under a Glass Bell* is burdened with Nin's past, and weighted with our own present, as it reenters the market today.

Notes

1. *The Diary of Anaïs Nin*, 3:115. All further quotations from the diary volumes 1 to 5 will be given in the text and identified by volume number and page.

2. Nin's main publications to date were *D. H. Lawrence: An Unprofessional Study; House of Incest;* and *Winter of Artifice.*

3. There were only eight stories in this first edition: "Houseboat," "The Mouse," "Under a Glass Bell," "The Mohican," "*Je suis le plus malade des Surréalistes*," "Ragtime," "The Labyrinth," and "Birth." The first commercial edition—by Dutton in 1948—includes the additional five titles we have here. For a history of the chronology of publication see Franklin. Stuhlmann explains in his foreword to the 1995 Swallow Press/Ohio University Press edition, reprinted in this 2014 edition: "The present edition of *Under a Glass Bell* contains all fifteen stories included in the enlarged Dutton edition of 1948." The Dutton edition included, in addition to the five new short stories, two novellas ("Djuna" and "The Voice"), for a total of fifteen. Note that Stuhlmann's own edition contains the thirteen stories but not the two novellas, and thus his "fifteen" must be a typo.

4. From Nin's unpublished diary, October 1943–March 1944. Quoted in Bair, 293.

5. For example, see Ardis and Lewis; Benstock; and Scott.

6. Published in the magazine *Matrix* 3, no. 3 (1941): 28–33 (Bair, 572n14).

7. Nin's interest in material book culture aligns her with writer and artist William Morris, a founder of the Arts and Crafts Movement in Britain in the 1860s, which sought, through its theories of design, to counter the impact of industrialization and to privilege traditional forms of craftsmanship. Morris created the Kelmscott Press in 1891 to publish limited-edition texts. Nin's comments about typesetting *Winter of Artifice* in January 1942 at the Gemor Press resonate with Morris's agenda: "The relationship to handcraft

is a beautiful one. . . . Gonzalo's love for first editions prepared him for good taste in design, in choosing type, paper, in spacing. . . . At the end of the day you can see your work, weigh it. It is done. It exists" (3:185–86). The Gemor Press further takes its place in book history alongside the Hogarth Press, originally a handpress founded by Virginia Woolf and her husband, Leonard Woolf, in 1917 (becoming part of Chatto & Windus in 1946); and the Gehenna Press, launched by American artist and designer Leonard Baskin in 1942.

Works Cited

Ardis, Ann L., and Leslie W. Lewis, eds. *Women's Experience of Modernity, 1875–1945*. Baltimore: Johns Hopkins University Press, 2003.

Bair, Deirdre. *Anaïs Nin: A Biography*. New York: G. P. Putnam's Sons, 1995.

Benstock, Shari. *Women of the Left Bank: Paris, 1900–1940*. Austin: University of Texas Press, 1986.

Cushman, Keith. "The View from Under a Glass Bell." *Mosaic: A Journal for the Comparative Study of Literature and Ideas* 11, no. 2 (January 1978): 109–19.

Mao, Douglas, and Rebecca L. Walkowitz. "The New Modernist Studies." *PMLA* 123, no. 3 (2008): 737–48.

Nin, Anaïs. *D. H. Lawrence: An Unprofessional Study*. Paris: Edward W. Titus, 1932.

———. *The Diary of Anaïs Nin*. Vol. 1, *1931–1934*. San Diego: Swallow Press and Harcourt, 1966.

———. *The Diary of Anaïs Nin*. Vol. 2, *1934–1939*. San Diego: Swallow Press and Harcourt Brace Jovanovich, 1967.

———. *The Diary of Anaïs Nin*. Vol. 3, *1939–1944*. San Diego: Harcourt Brace Jovanovich, 1969.

———. *The Diary of Anaïs Nin*. Vol. 4, *1944–1947*. New York: Harcourt Brace Jovanovich, 1971.

———. *The Diary of Anaïs Nin*. Vol. 5, *1947–1955*. San Diego: Harcourt Brace Jovanovich, 1974.

———. *House of Incest*. Paris: Siana Editions, 1936.

———. *Incest: The Unexpurgated Diary of Anaïs Nin, 1932–1934*. New York: Harcourt Brace Jovanovich, 1992.

———. *The Novel of the Future*. Athens: Swallow Press/Ohio University Press, 1968.

———. *Winter of Artifice*. Paris: The Obelisk Press, 1939.

Franklin, Benjamin, V. "Noli Me Tangere: The Structure of Anais Nin's *Under a Glass Bell*." *Studies in Short Fiction* 34, no. 4 (Fall 1997): 459–79.

Scholar, Nancy. "Anaïs Nin Under a Glass Bell." *Michigan Quarterly Review* 20, no. 3 (1981): 308–12.

Scott, Bonnie Kime, ed. *The Gender of Modernism: A Critical Anthology*. Bloomington: Indiana University Press, 1990.

Stuhlmann, Gunther. Foreword to *Under a Glass Bell and Other Stories*, by Anaïs Nin, vii–xviii. Athens: Swallow Press/Ohio University Press, 1995.

Woolf, Virginia. *A Room of One's Own*. London: Grafton, 1977.

Foreword to the 1995 Swallow Press Edition

GUNTHER STUHLMANN

In February 1944, or shortly thereafter, there appeared in Frances Steloff's Gotham Book Mart in New York, and in a few other literary venues, an elegantly printed volume of less than one hundred pages, enhanced by a series of black and white line engravings. It bore the title *Under a Glass Bell*, and contained eight brief stories by Anaïs Nin. On the last page the book carried a note from its publisher: "This edition is limited to three hundred copies. It has been handset by the author in Bernhard Gothic Light Italic, ten point, printed on watermarked Zurich Plate Finish Paper. Design, typography and printing by the Gemor Press. The cover and seventeen engravings by Ian Hugo have been printed in relief directly from the original copper plates." A few months later, in June 1944, the Gemor Press produced a second edition of *Under a Glass Bell*. This time the print run was listed as limited to eight hundred copies. The typeface had been changed and only nine of Ian Hugo's engravings had been reproduced, again directly from the original plates. Altogether, this was the largest number of copies of a single work produced by Anaïs Nin's Gemor Press since its inception in 1942, when, with a few hundred borrowed dollars, she had acquired an ancient, rickety, foot-pedaled printing press and a few boxes of type she had learned, by trial and error, to set by hand, letter by letter, thirty-three lines to a page, one page a day. It also was the largest number of copies printed of any of her published works. And, as it turned out, it seems to have marked, at long last, a turning point in her literary fortune in the United States.

When the outbreak of World War II had forced Anaïs Nin and her husband, Hugh Guiler (who presented his artistic work under the pseudonym Ian Hugo), to return to New York late in 1939, after having lived in France for some fifteen years, she had noted in her diary: "We all knew we were parting from a pattern of life we would never see again, from friends we might never see again. I knew it was the end of our romantic life."

Anaïs Nin's renewed confrontation with America at the beginning of the 1940s echoed in some ways the sentiments she had expressed when she arrived for the first time in New York harbor on the S.S. *Montserrat* in August 1914, clutching her brother's violin case to distinguish herself as an "artist" from the other hapless Spanish immigrants faced with the prospect of having to establish a new life in a new and strange country. Her childhood in Europe, which appeared so enchanted in retrospect, had been abruptly terminated by her father's desertion of the family. At the age of eleven she had found New York "too big, too superficial, everything goes too fast." But she had vowed to be brave, to keep her negative thoughts to herself, to confide them only to the diary she had begun to write during her journey into exile, into an uncertain future.

Twenty-five years later, on the surface of her life, Anaïs Nin once again embraced the myriad activities of the city which during her occasional visits in the 1930s had seemed so alive to her, so jazzy, compared to the decaying capitals of Europe and their weary inhabitants. In her teens she had ransacked the public library shelves to educate herself on her own, to adopt English as her language, to overcome her sense of isolation from ordinary—especially American—life by seeking refuge in literature, in writing. Now she set out to build upon the small body of work she had so determinedly created in France: her study of D. H. Lawrence, the two volumes of fictions—*The House of Incest* and *The Winter of Artifice*—and the handful of stories that had appeared scattered about in little magazines. She had in fact become the artist she had once pretended to be.

But in the confidential pages of her ongoing diary she once again deplored the overpowering impact of the city, its conspicuous consumption, its aggressive commercialism and the absence of a human dimension in daily life. "Where are the cafés with only three small tables and tottering chairs?" she asked. She missed "the tender human scale of Paris." She did not respond to "Gulliver's country," to "giant scales." "Great sadness last night," she recorded on New Year's Day 1940. "All around us there is excitement in place of exaltation, rush and action in place of depth, humor in place of feeling."

Most disappointing, perhaps, there was little response to her writing among the publishers she approached, the editors of conventional magazines, the left-leaning, hardnosed intellectuals of the New York literary establishment. A few copies of the books she had published in France in the 1930s in minuscule editions (five hundred and fifty copies of *D. H. Lawrence: An Unprofessional Study*, two hundred and forty-nine copies of *The House of Incest*) had found their way to the ever-supportive Gotham Book Mart in New York. A few had been sent to friendly subscribers who had initially helped to defray their printing cost. Most copies of *The Winter of Artifice* had unaccountably vanished in the turmoil following the sudden death of her publisher, Jack Kahane, the demise of his Obelisk Press, and the outbreak of war on September 1, 1939. Only two of her stories had appeared, in 1938, in small American literary magazines edited by personal friends, in James Cooney's *The Phoenix* and Dorothy Norman's *Twice a Year*. And throughout the 1930s she had tried in vain to interest American editors, from H. L. Mencken to Maxwell Perkins, in her writing. Among the New York literati Anaïs Nin was known, perhaps, as a somewhat intriguing, mysterious female character rather than recognized as a writer, or at best dismissed as a sort of European "surrealist" whose preoccupation with "dreams" and psychological subtleties, with "poetic" prose, were marginal and esoteric. Instead of frivolous, narcissistic fantasies, she had been told, write something substantial like *The Good Earth*. Even Alfred Perlès, her Parisian admirer and *copain*, in the only review of the original edition of *The Winter of Artifice*, which appeared in an obscure magazine, *Purpose*, in 1940, did not help her cause very much, one suspects, when he called it "one of the strangest books I have ever read," a book written as if by "some nereid or dryad—atmospheric and seasonal."

❦ ❦ ❦ ❦

By 1942 Anaïs Nin had decided to take her literary fate into her own hands. Her diary in those years reflects both anger and de-fiance. "Literature, the ultimate gift for expressing the most subtle aspects of man's thought and feeling," she wrote, "may not sur-vive persecution: first by religion, then by the bourgeoisie, then by Marxism, and now by commercialism." She also wrote: "It wasn't enough for me to weep every day because there was war. I felt that you had to create an antidote, you had to create another world . . . and that was called escapism."

Her antidote to the rejection of her work was to establish a small press, in her studio at 144 Macdougal Street in Manhattan, named after her collaborator, Gonzalo Moré, the "Gemor Press." Gonzalo, the Peruvian communist and artist-*manqué* with whom she had fallen in love in Paris years ago, had also found a temporary refuge in New York by then. Neither of them was experienced in setting type by hand, in inking and feeding the foot-cranked letter press, sheet by sheet, with the remnants of exquisite paper that they had picked up at bargain prices. But for Anaïs Nin it was the realization of a long-held dream that began in the early 1930s, in the old house in Louveciennes, when she and Henry Miller had hoped to print their own "unpublishable" works on their own press in a loft above the garage. "The creation of an individual world," she wrote in her diary in January 1943, "an act of independence, such as the work on the press, is a marvelous cure for anger and frustration. The insults of publishers, the rejections, the ignorance, all are forgotten."

The first product of Anaïs Nin's defiant, labor-intensive enter-prise was a handsome, revised edition of *Winter of Artifice*. Unlike the Paris original, it contained only two novellas, both extensively rewritten: "Lillith," also known as the "father story" then retitled "Winter of Artifice," became the title story of all later editions, and "The Voice," drawn from the diary record of her lay-therapist days in New York in 1934–1935. Missing was "Djuna," the novella so transparently based on the actual diary pages capturing her initial involvement with Henry Miller and his seductive second wife, June, which in Anaïs Nin's new American circumstances might have been dangerously indiscreet. In fact, it was never reprinted during her lifetime. The book appeared in the summer of 1942, in an edition of five hundred copies. It included a handful of original engravings by her husband. Obviously proud of the first result of her adventure in the printing trade, Anaïs Nin included a note that the volume had been "set by hand and printed by the author in Spartan type of twelve points on Copper Plate Paper." And she informed the reader that the copper engravings had been created using the technique "which William Blake called 'revealed' because it was revealed to him by his brother in a dream. This is the first time this technique, as developed by S. W. Hayter, has been employed since Blake invented it."

The book and its production, of course, elicited a great deal of praise from friends and admirers of Anaïs Nin's work. It also received three reviews in New York, in respectable publications—*The New York Herald Tribune, The Nation,* and in *New Directions #7*—by respected writers, among them Paul Rosenfeld and William Carlos Williams. Anaïs Nin, apparently, had hoped for more. "The silence around *Winter of Artifice* distresses me," she noted in January 1943. "No reviews."

But by the summer of that year she was "gathering strength" for another project, a collection of stories to be called, after one of these, *Under a Glass Bell.* In June, Gonzalo Moré had begun designing "a beautiful book." By October she had set 35 pages of type, collected 56 subscriptions, and printed the first page. Early in 1944, the first copies were ready.

❖ ❖ ❖ ❖

Anaïs Nin's new life in New York, it seems, provided more dissatisfactions at first than heightened moments which might have served as springboards for new artistic creations. Thus it was not surprising that she began to reach back to the pattern of life, to the friends she had been forced to leave behind. "I saw my life in Paris with the added elements of fiction: lighting, focus, the gold patina which memory adds to it and they appear to me more vividly," she noted. "They are highlighted in this case by poignant memory and a desire to relive it all, now that it is forever lost."

Already shortly after her return Anaïs Nin had begun to re-capture some of the facets of her past life. She had worked on the story of her houseboat, the *Belle Aurore*, combining sharply observed diary material, the reflections of actual events, with the transforming symbolic elements of a dream journey she had explored once in an early, unpublished story, "Waste of Timelessness." "The artist deals in symbols," she had stated in the diary, "that is: reality illumined by the soul." As always, her "fairy tale"—as she called all of her fictions based on the bedrock reality of her diary—was anchored in a "real" world of *clochards*, prostitutes, bored policemen, in the pal-pable, tarred beams of the old barge with its banging shutters and the fancy Arabian bedstead, interwoven with the delicate fabric of her imaginings. And the dream-boat life was terminated again by an actual, as well as symbolic, event: the arrival, fleetingly, of George VI on a ceremonial state visit, which gave the "river police" the chance to rid the heart of Paris of the ramshackle, Depression-era barges that lined the quays of the Seine. Indeed, it may have been the "reality" of the ending of the house-boat story which prompted the small Phila-delphia magazine, *Matrix*, where the story first appeared in 1941, to call it "I'll Never Forgive the King of England."

Sitting on a bench in Washington Square in September 1940, Anaïs Nin had begun what she initially called the "Story of Pierre," interweaving intimate diary material reflecting her involvement with the erratic poet of the theater Antonin Artaud, eventually, with an earlier story which seemed to provide the perfect climax for her por-trait of the *plus malade* of the surrealists. A brief sketch written in French, "Le Merle Blanc," recreating the atmosphere of a madhouse she had visited with a friend in Paris, had appeared in *The Booster*, Henry Miller and Alfred Perlès's iconoclastic magazine, in 1937. It now served to provide the image symbolizing the deranged institu-tional world in which her friend Artaud had become incarcerated in the late 1930s. The story, Anaïs Nin wrote, was "a composite of real fragments from the diary and imaginary conversations." In the same way she fashioned the portraits of other friends who had enriched or challenged her life in France: Louise de Vilmorin, encapsulated in the incestuous amber of her aristocratic glass-house life; Conrad Moricand, the always impeccable down-at-the-heels astrologer, "who could not distinguish between the dream and the actuality"; the anonymous French servant girl whose unwanted pregnancy echoed Anaïs Nin's own traumatic experience with angry doctors "baffled as before a savage mystery," as she had written in her own "Birth" story, first published in 1938.

Of the eight stories gathered in the first edition of *Under a Glass Bell* in 1944, two dated back, also, to Anaïs Nin's tentative beginnings as a published writer. A friend of Lawrence Durrell's, Nicholas Moore, editor of the English magazine *Seven*, in the autumn of 1938, had published "Ragtime." In her diary its genesis had been an ultimately fruitless search to find a gypsy caravan that could be rented and serve as a shelter for a loving couple. But in her story Anaïs Nin had transformed the scene at the outskirts of Paris into a timeless, poetic fable that told us that—as in her own memory—"nothing is lost but it changes."

"The Labyrinth," originally entitled "The Paper Womb," had appeared in the winter 1937/1938 issue of *The Booster*, as part of its irreverent "Air-conditioned Womb Number," which bore on its title page the inscription: "The Labyrinth / The Plinth / The Nth/ By the Womb Sextette," composed of Miller, Nin, Perlès, William Saroyan, Durrell, and the mysterious "Le Huitan."

❖ ❖ ❖ ❖

A few months before *Under a Glass Bell* appeared in New York, Anaïs Nin had written in her diary: "The guilt the poet has carried for working out his individual patterns and pleasures separately from the rest of the world is reflected in his anxiety and loneliness." Given the temper of the times, a horrendous war raging in Europe and in the Pacific, the political engagement of many of her friends, and the dim reception of her work in America, she apparently felt the need to defend her art, for she added a "Foreword" to the first edition of *Under a Glass Bell*:

These stories represent the moment when many like myself had found only one answer to the suffering of the world: to dream, to tell fairy-tales, to elaborate and to follow the labyrinths of fantasy. All this I see now was the passive poet's only answer to the torments he witnessed . . . The Spanish War awakened me. I passed out of romanticism, mysticism and neurosis into reality . . . I am in the difficult position of presenting stories which are dreams and of having to say: But now, although I give you these, I am awake! Some may say: Then why don't you publish your new writing and give us your new awareness? The answer to this I can best make through a story.

I once saw a Russian film of dancers. One was a Mongolian woman most elaborately dressed in gold embroideries, with tasselled jewelry on her forehead, bells on her ankles and wrists. This was the traditional feast costume. However, this Mongolian dancer was a Soviet and wanting to express the new spirit she felt she decided to do the "Dance of the Girl Sewing in the Factory." In this elaborate *accoutrement*, the sediment of centuries of aesthetic refinements, she made the gestures of the girl sewing in a factory, occasionally forgetting her theme and shaking her shoulders and eyes in the old bizarre manner. Not wishing to be like this dancer I am merely presenting these dream dances while I change my costume.

It soon became evident, however, that *Under a Glass Bell* did not need to be defended against a phalanx of hostile critics—there was no public critical response to the book. Her friends reacted positively. "You represent our poetic soul," a Marxist friend told her, according to her *Diary*, "and I regret having talked to you last summer about objective writing. I see now that you have to go on being the poet for all of us." An English critic disagreed with her defense of her position as a "dreamer." "You underestimate the possibilities of your dreams embracing the *Zeitgeist*," he wrote to her. "If they are good dreams they will do that. And your dreams are good. 'Birth' is a beautiful and terrifying story." And he added: "The 'Houseboat' is, or was, truly . . . the individualist's hide-out which is no hide-out at all. You know that."

The only critic who responded to the book in print, of course, was Edmund Wilson, the then *éminence grise* of American letters. His review in *The New Yorker* suddenly legitimized Anaïs Nin as a serious writer and, eventually, led to her first connection with the heretofore elusive world of commercial New York publishing. Wilson declared that he had been somewhat disappointed by the snippets from the much rumored about but still unpublished diary which had appeared scattered in little magazines and in their *Winter of Artifice* disguises—"those rather fragmentary examples of a kind of autobiographical fantasy" as he called them. But he had kinder words for *Under a Glass Bell*. "The pieces in this collection belong to a peculiar genre sometimes cultivated by the late Virginia Woolf," he wrote in the issue of April 1, 1944. "They are half short stories, half dreams, and they mix a sometimes exquisite poetry with a homely realistic observation. They take place in a special world, in a world of feminine perception and fancy, which is all the more curious and charming for being innocently international." Unlike the other literary surrealists, among whom Wilson obviously counted her for lack of any other categorization, he concluded "Miss Nin is a very good artist."

Four years later, when the first commercial edition of *Under a Glass Bell* appeared under the E. P. Dutton imprint, it had been enriched with five additional stories, and bulked up with the two novelettes of the reworked *Winter of Artifice*. The book was dedicated "To Gonzalo Moré, who designed a limited edition of my work and who by his art in printing and typography contributed to its success." But it no longer contained her apologetic foreword, which had been included in a British edition in 1947, and which has never been used or reprinted since.

❖ ❖ ❖ ❖

The present [1995] edition of *Under a Glass Bell* contains all fifteen [actually, thirteen] stories included in the enlarged Dutton edition of 1948. They have been rearranged [in the 1995 edition] to reflect, to some extent, the sequence of events and persons recorded in the diary which served as their inspiration rather than the uncertain chronological order in which they were written or published.

While there are subtle changes in style, in the deployment of the "raw" material underlying each story, which may allow us to chart and date Anaïs Nin's progress as a writer during the decade in which these stories took shape, her initial artistic and emotional vision never seems to have faltered. It is always evident, it remains sharply focused. Of the five stories added in 1948 to the original collection, some represent additional portraits of other Parisian friends she had to leave behind: The "all-seeing" Jean Carteret, who had introduced her to the madhouse in Paris; the imagist German refugee painter Hans Reichel. These portraits had appeared, meanwhile, in little magazines edited again by friends, like Wolfgang Paalen's *Dyn* in Mexico, and George Leite's *Circle* in Berkeley, California. "A Child Born Out of the Fog" had first been printed, in July 1947, as an eight-page pamphlet by a combative Anaïs Nin herself. In an "Editor's Note" in the Gemor Press edition she stated: "This little sketch which is here first presented to the public, is being published in this form because we agree with the magazine editors who pronounced it 'exquisitely written,' while questioning their dictum that 'because of its subject matter its publication at this time would not be wise.'" In the late 1940s in America, an "inter-racial" couple having a child, of course, was a touchy subject, as touchy perhaps as abortion, which had prompted Anaïs Nin, one suspects, to change some of the "real" circumstances of the experience on which her "Birth" story had been based. "Hedja," the unveiling of woman, had initially been a separate part of another Gemor Press edition, *This Hunger*, published in 1945.

✦ ✦ ✦ ✦

In October 1943, Anaïs Nin had written in her *Diary:* "My stories need to be placed in their light and time to be understood. They were written before the war. The fact that I describe adult fairy tales, the fantasy, does not mean that I remain permanently with them . . . I am no longer in this world I describe." But as this collection made its precarious way through the minefields of commercial publishing, going out of print, being resurrected by her never quite flagging spirit, long after the demise of the Gemor Press, Anaïs Nin eventually reached the point where she no longer felt compelled to apologize for her fairy tales, her dreams, her fantasies. Introducing a new British edition of *Under a Glass Bell* in 1968 she wrote: ". . . these stories broke a mold and used the distillation of poetry. My journals supply the key to the mythical figures and assert the reality of what once may have seemed to be purely fantasy. Such a marriage of illusion and reality—or illusion as the key to reality—is a contemporary theme."

In the midst of World War II, her British friend had assured Anaïs Nin that her social conscience, her concern for human suffering, was deeply etched into her fantasies, perhaps more effectively than what could be found in the propagandistic rhetoric of the day. A story like "The Mouse," he wrote, belonged "as much to the present war ethos as it does to an esoteric, seemingly timeless problem." The bleeding, frightened French servant girl, spurned by society on account of her pregnancy was kin "to the bewildered, adolescent girl in the blackout, or the lonely, demoralized wife, or even those near soldiers' camps who gave themselves up to an unsatisfactory ritual of love for a bar of soap or a tin of corned beef." Even without the key of the diary, it seems, readers were able to respond to Anaïs Nin's poetic distillations.

In April 1944, after the first three hundred copies of her little book had been loosed upon the world, Anaïs Nin felt compelled to write in her *Diary:* "The connection I made with a few people from the publication of *Under a Glass Bell* seemed like the breaking of a shell (how many shells?), a second birth (how many births?), a becoming visible and tangible. My feeling of being merely a mysterious influence upon others ceased. I felt out in the daylight."

Becket, Massachusetts, Summer 1994
Gunther Stuhlmann

UNDER A GLASS BELL

Houseboat

The current of the crowd wanted to sweep me along with it. The green lights on the street corners ordered me to cross the street, the policeman smiled to invite me to walk between the silver-headed nails. Even the autumn leaves obeyed the current. But I broke away from it like a fallen piece. I swerved out and stood at the top of the stairs leading down to the Quays. Below me flowed the river. Not like the current I had just broken from, made of dissonant pieces colliding rustily, driven by hunger and desire.

Down the stairs I ran towards the water front, the noises of the city receding as I descended, the leaves retreating to the corner of the steps under the wind of my skirt. At the bottom of the stairs lay the wrecked mariners of the street current, the tramps who had fallen out of the crowd life, who refused to obey. Like me, at some point of the trajectory, they had all fallen out, and here they lay shipwrecked at the foot of the trees, sleeping, drinking. They had abandoned time, possessions, labor, slavery. They walked and slept in counter-rhythm to the world. They renounced houses and clothes. They sat alone, but not unique, for they all seemed to have been born brothers. Time and exposure made their clothes alike, wine and air gave them the same eroded skin. The crust of dirt, the swollen noses, the stale tears in the eyes, all gave them the same appearance. Having refused to follow the procession of the streets, they sought the river which lulled them. Wine and water. Every day, in front of the river, they reenacted the ritual of abandon. Against the knots of rebellion, wine and the river, against the cutting iron of loneliness, wine and water washing away everything in a rhythm of blurred silences.

They threw the newspapers into the river and this was their prayer: to be carried, lifted, borne down, without feeling the hard bone of pain in man, lodged in his skeleton, but only the pulse of flowing blood. No shocks, no violence, no awakening.

While the tramps slept, the fishermen in a trance pretended to be capturing fish, and stood there hypnotized for hours. The river communicated with them through the bamboo rods of their fishing tackle, transmitting its vibrations. Hunger and time were forgotten. The perpetual waltz of lights and shadows emptied one of all memories and terrors. Fishermen, tramps, filled by the brilliance of the river as by an anesthetic which permitted only the pulse to beat, emptied of memories as in dancing.

The houseboat was tied at the foot of the stairs. Broad and heavy on its keel, stained with patches of lights and shadows, bathing in reflections, it heaved now and then to the pressure of a deeper breathing of the river. The water washed its flanks lingeringly, the moss gathered around the base of it, just below the water line, and swayed like Naiad hair, then folded back again in silky adherence to the wood. The shutters opened and closed in obedience to the gusts of wind and the heavy poles which kept the barge from touching the shore cracked with the strain like bones. A shiver passed along the houseboat asleep on the river, like a shiver of fever in a dream. The lights and shadows stopped waltzing. The nose of the houseboat plunged deeper and shook its chains. A moment of anguish: everything was slipping into anger again, as on earth. But no, the water dream persisted. Nothing was displaced. The nightmare might appear here, but the river knew the mystery of continuity. A fit of anger and only the surface erupted, leaving the deep flowing body of the dream intact.

The noises of the city receded completely as I stepped on the gangplank. As I took out the key I felt nervous. If the key fell into the river, the key to the little door to my life in the infinite? Or if the houseboat broke its moorings and floated away? It had done this once already, breaking the chain at the prow, and the tramps had helped to swing it back in place.

As soon as I was inside of the houseboat, I no longer knew the name of the river or the city. Once inside the walls of old wood, under the heavy beams, I might be inside a Norwegian sailing ship traversing fjords, in a Dutch boyer sailing to Bali, a jute boat on the Brahmaputra. At night the lights on the shore were those of Constantinople or the Neva. The giant bells ringing the hours were those of the Sunken Cathedral. Every time I inserted the key in the lock, I felt this snapping of cords, this lifting of anchor, this fever of departure. Once inside the houseboat, all the voyages began. Even at night with its shutters closed, no smoke coming out of its chimney, asleep and secret, it had an air of mysteriously sailing somewhere.

At night I closed the windows which overlooked the Quays. As I leaned over I could see dark shadows walking by, men with their collars turned up and their caps pushed over their eyes, women with wide long skirts, market women who made love with the tramps behind the trees. The street lamps high above threw no light on the trees and bushes along the big wall. It was only when the window rustled that the shadows which seemed to be one shadow split into two swiftly and then, in the silence, melted into one again.

At this moment a barge full of coal passed by, sent waves rolling behind it, upheaving all the other barges. The pictures on the walls swayed. The fishing net hung on the ceiling like a giant spider web swung, gently rocking a sea shell and a starfish caught in its meshes.

On the table lay a revolver. No harm could come to me on the water but someone had laid a revolver there believing I might need it. I looked at it as if it reminded me of a crime I had committed, with an irrepressible smile such as rises sometimes to people's lips in the face of great catastrophes which are beyond their grasp, the smile which comes at times on certain women's faces while they are saying they regret the harm they have done. It is the smile of nature quietly and proudly asserting its natural right to kill, the smile which the animal in the jungle never shows but by which man reveals when the animal re-enters his being and reasserts its presence. This smile came to me as I took up the revolver and pointed it out of the window, into the river. But I was so averse to killing that even shooting into the water I felt uneasy, as if I might kill the Unknown Woman of the Seine again—the woman who had drowned herself here years ago and who was so beautiful that at the Morgue they had taken a plaster cast of her face. The shot came faster than I had expected. The river swallowed it. No one noticed it, not from the bridge, not from the Quays. How easily a crime could be committed here.

Outside an old man was playing the violin feverishly, but no sound came out of it. He was deaf. No music poured from his instrument, no music, but tiny plaintive cries escaped from his trembling gestures.

At the top of the stairs two policemen were chatting with the prostitutes.

The windows overlooking the Quays now shut, the barge looked uninhabited. But the windows looking on the river were open. The dying summer breath entered into my bedroom, the room of shadows, the bower of the night. Heavy beams overhead, low ceilings, a heavy wooden sideboard along the walls. An Indian lamp threw charcoal patterns over walls and ceiling—a Persian design of cactus flowers, lace fans, palm leaves, a lamaist vajry-mandala flower, minarets, trellises.

(When I lie down to dream, it is not merely a dust flower born like a rose out of the desert sands and destroyed by a gust of wind. When I lie down to dream it is to plant the seed for the miracle and the fulfillment.)

The headboard opened like a fan over my head, a peacock feather opening in dark wood and copper threads, the wings of a great golden bird kept afloat on the river. The barge could sink, but not this wide heavy bed traveling throughout the nights spread over the deepest precipices of desire. Falling on it I felt the waves of emotion which sustained me, the constant waves of emotion under my feet. Burrowing myself into the bed only to spread fanwise and float into a moss-carpeted tunnel of caresses.

The incense was spiraling. The candles were burning with delicate oscillations of anguish. Watching them was like listening to a beloved heartbeat and fearing the golden hammer strokes might stop. The candles never conquered the darkness but maintained a disquieting duel with the night.

I heard a sound on the river, but when I leaned out of the window the river had become silent again. Now I heard the sound of oars. Softly, softly coming from the shore. A boat knocked against the barge. There was a sound of chains being tied.

I await the phantom lover—the one who haunts all women, the one I dream of, who stands behind every man, with a finger and head shaking—"Not him, he is not the one." Forbidding me each time to love.

✤ ✤ ✤ ✤

The houseboat must have traveled during the night, the climate and the scenery were changed. Dawn was accelerated by a woman's shrieks. Shrieks interrupted by the sound of choking. I ran on deck. I arrived just as the woman who was drowning grasped the anchor's chain. Her shrieks grew worse as she felt nearer salvation, her appetite for life growing more violent. With the help of one of the drunken tramps, we pulled the chain up, with the woman clinging to it. She was hiccuping, spitting, choking. The drunken tramp was shouting orders to imaginary sailors, telling them what to do for the drowned. Leaning over the woman he almost toppled over her, which reawakened her aggressiveness and helped her to rise and walk into the barge where we changed her clothes.

The barge was traversing a dissonant climate. The mud had come to the surface of the river, and a shoal of corks surrounded the barge. We pushed them away with brooms and poles; the corks seemed to catch the current and float away, only to encircle the barge magnetically.

The tramps were washing themselves at the fountain. Bare to the waist, they soaked their faces and shoulders, and then they washed their shirts, and combed themselves, dipping their combs in the river. These men at the fountain, they knew what was going to happen. When they saw me on deck, they gave me the news of the day, of the approach of war, of the hope of revolution. I listened to their description of tomorrow's world. An aurora borealis and all men out of prison.

The oldest tramp of all, who did not know about tomorrow, he was in the prison of his drunkenness. No escape. When he was filled like a barrel, then his legs gave way and he could only fall down. When he was lifted by alcoholic wings and ready for flight, the wings collapsed into nausea. This gangplank of drunkenness led nowhere.

The same day at this post of anguish, three men quarreled on the Quays. One carried a ragpicker's bag over his shoulder. The second was brilliantly elegant. The third was a beggar with a wooden leg. They argued excitedly. The elegant one was counting out money. He dropped a ten-franc piece. The beggar placed his wooden leg on it and would not budge. No one could frighten him, and no one dared to push off the wooden leg. He kept it there all the time they argued. Only when the two others went off did he lean over to pick it up.

The street cleaner was sweeping the dead leaves into the river. The rain fell into the cracked letter box and when I opened my letters it looked as if my friends had been weeping when writing me.

A child sat on the edge of the river, his thin legs dangling. He sat there for two or three hours and then began to cry. The street cleaner asked him what was the matter. His mother had told him) to wait there until she returned. She had left him a piece of dry bread. He was wearing his little black school apron. The street cleaner took his comb, dipped it in the river and combed the child's hair and washed his face. I offered to take him on the barge. The street cleaner said: "She'll never come back. That's how they do it. He's another for the Orphanage."

When the child heard the word orphanage he ran away so fast the street cleaner did not have time to drop his broom. He shrugged his shoulders: "They'll catch him sooner or later. I was one of them."

Voyage of despair.

The river was having a nightmare. Its vast whaleback was restless. It had been cheated of its daily suicide. More women fed the river than men—more wanted to die in winter than in summer.

Parasitic corks obeyed every undulation but did not separate from the barge, glued like waves of mercury. When it rained the water seeped through the top room and fell on my bed, on my books, on the black rug.

I awakened in the middle of the night with wet hair. I thought I must be at the bottom of the Seine; that the barge, the bed, had quietly sunk during the night.

It was not very different to look through water at all things. It was like weeping cool saltless tears without pain. I was not cut off altogether, but in so deep a region that every element was marrying in sparkling silence, so deep that I heard the music of the spinet in-side the snail who carries his antennae like an organ and travels on the back of a harp fish.

In this silence and white communion took place the convo-lutions of plants turning into flesh, into planets. The towers were pierced by swordfishes, the moon of citron rotated on a sky of lava, the branches had thirsty eyes hanging like berries. Tiny birds sat on weeds asking for no food and singing no song but the soft chant of metamor-phosis, and each time they opened their beaks the webbed stained-glass windows decomposed into snakes and ribbons of sulphur.

The light filtered through the slabs of mildewed tombs and no eyelashes could close against it, no tears could blur it, no eyelids could curtain it off, no sleep could dissolve it, no forgetfulness could deliver one from this place where there was neither night nor day. Fish, plant, woman, equally aware, with eyes forever open, con-founded and confused in communion, in an ecstasy without repose.

I ceased breathing in the present, inhaling the air around me into the leather urns of the lungs. I breathed out into the infinite, exhaling the mist of a three-quarter-tone breath, a light pyramid of heart beats.

This breathing lighter than breathing, without pressure from the wind, like the windless delicacy of the air in Chinese paintings, supporting one winged black bird, one breathless cloud, bowing one branch, preceded the white hysteria of the poet and the red-foamed hysteria of woman.

When this inhaling of particles, of dust grains, of rust microbes, of all the ashes of past deaths ceased, I inhaled the air from the unborn and felt my body like a silk scarf resting outside the blue rim of the nerves.

The body recovered the calm of minerals, its plant juices, the eyes became gems again, made to glitter alone and not for the shed-ding of tears.

Sleep.

No need to watch the flame of my life in the palm of my hand, this flame as pale as the holy ghost speaking in many languages to which none have the secret.

The dream will watch over it. No need to remain with eyes wide open. Now the eyes are gems, the hair a fan of lace. Sleep is upon me.

The pulp of roots, the milk of cactus, the quicksilver drippings of the silver beeches is in my veins.

I sleep with my feet on moss carpets, my branches in the cotton of the clouds.

The sleep of a hundred years has transfixed all into the silver face of ecstasy.

✤ ✤ ✤ ✤

During the night the houseboat traveled out of the landscape of despair. Sunlight struck the wooden beams, and the reflected light of the water danced on the wooden beams. Opening my eyes I saw the light playing around me and I felt as if I were looking through a pierced sky into some region far nearer to the sun. Where had the houseboat sailed to during the night?

The island of joy must be near. I leaned out of the window. The moss costume of the houseboat was greener, washed by cleaner waters. The corks were gone, and the smell of rancid wine. The little waves passed with great precipitation. The waves were so clear I could see the roots of the indolent algae plants that had grown near the edge of the river.

This day I landed at the island of joy.

I could now put around my neck the sea-shell necklace and walk through the city with the arrogance of my secret.

When I returned to the houseboat with my arms loaded with new candles, wine, ink, writing paper, nails for the broken shutters, the policeman stopped me at the top of the stairs: "Is there a holiday on the Quay?"

"A holiday? No."

As I ran down the stairs I understood. There was a holiday on the Quay! The policeman had seen it on my face. A celebration of lights and motion. Confetti of sun spots, serpentines of water currents, music from the deaf violinist. It was the island of joy I had touched in the morning. The river and I united in a long, winding, never-ending dream, with its deep undercurrents, its deeper undertows of dark activity, the river and I rejoicing at teeming obscure mysteries of river-bottom lives.

The big clock of the Sunken Cathedral rang twelve times for the feast. Barges passed slowly in the sun, like festive chariots throwing bouquets of lightning from their highly polished knobs. The laundry in blue, white and rose, hung out to dry and waving like flags, children playing with cats and dogs, women holding the rudder with serenity and gravity. Everything washed clean with water and light passing at a dream pace.

But when I reached the bottom of the stairs the festivity came to an abrupt end. Three men were cutting the algae plants with long scythes. I shouted but they worked on unconcerned, pushing them all away so that the current would sweep them off. The men laughed at my anger. One man said: "These are not your plants. Cleaning Department order. Go and complain to them." And with quicker gestures they cut all the algae and fed the limp green carpet to the current.

So passed the barge out of the island of joy.

✤ ✤ ✤ ✤

One morning what I found in the letter box was an order from the river police to move on. The King of England was expected for a visit and he would not like the sight of the houseboats, the laundry exposed on the decks, the chimneys and water tanks in rusty colors, the gangplanks with teeth missing, and other human flowers born of poverty and laziness. We were all ordered to sail on, quite a way up the Seine, no one knew quite where because it was all in technical language.

One of my neighbors, a one-eyed cyclist, came to discuss the dispossessions and to invoke laws which had not been made to give houseboats the right to lie in the heart of Paris gathering moss. The fat painter who lived across the river, open-shirted and always perspiring, came to discuss the matter and to suggest we not move at all as a form of protest. What could happen? At the worst, since there were no laws against our staying, the police would have to fetch a tugboat and move us all in a line, like a row of prisoners. That was the worst that could happen to us. But the one-eyed cyclist was overcome by this threat because he said his houseboat was not strong enough to bear the strain of being pulled between other heavier, larger barges. He had heard of a small houseboat being wrenched apart in such a voyage. He did not think mine would stand the strain either.

The next day the one-eyed man was towed along by a friend who ran one of the tourist steamers; he left at dawn like a thief, with his fear of collective moving. Then the fat painter moved, pulled heavily and slowly because his barge was the heaviest. He owned a piano and huge canvases, heavier than coal. His leaving left a vast hole in the alignment of barges, like a tooth missing. The fishermen crowded in this open space to fish and rejoiced. They had been wishing us away, and I believe it was their prayers which were heard rather than ours, for soon the letters from the police became more insistent.

I was the last one left, still believing I would be allowed to stay. Every morning I went to see the chief of police. I always believed an exception would be made for me, that laws and regulations broke down for me. I don't know why except that I had seen it happen very often. The chief of police was extremely hospitable; he permitted me to sit in his office for hours and gave me pamphlets to pass the time. I became versed in the history of the Seine. I knew the number of sunken barges, collided Sunday tourist steamboats, of people saved from suicide by the river police. But the law remained adamant, and the advice of the chief of police, on the sly, was for me to take my houseboat to a repair yard near Paris where I could have a few re-pairs made while waiting for permission to return. The yard being near Paris, I made arrangements for a tugboat to come for me in the middle of the day.

The tugboat's approach to the barge was very much like a court-ship, made with great care and many cork protectors. The tugboat knew the fragility of these discarded barges converted into house-boats. The wife of the tugboat captain was cooking lunch while the maneuvers were carried out. The sailors were untying the ropes, one

was stoking the fire. When the tugboat and the barge were tied together like twins, the captain lifted the gangplank, opened his bottle
of red wine, drank a very full gulp and gave orders for departure.

Now we were gliding along. I was running all over the houseboat, celebrating the strangest sensation I had ever known, this traveling along a river with all my possessions around me, my books, my
diaries, my furniture, my pictures, my clothes in the closet. I leaned
out of each little window to watch the landscape. I lay on the bed. It
was a dream. It was a dream, this being a marine snail traveling with
one's house all around one's neck.

A marine snail gliding through the familiar city. Only in a dream
could I move so gently along with the small human heartbeat in
rhythm with the tug tug heartbeat of the tugboat, and Paris unfolding, uncurling, in beautiful undulations.

The tugboat pulled its smokestacks down to pass under the
first bridge. The captain's wife was serving lunch on deck. Then I
discovered with anxiety that the barge was taking in water. It had
already seeped through the floor. I began to work the pumps, but
could not keep abreast of the leaks. Then I filled pails, pots and pans,
and still I could not control the water, so I called out to the captain.
He laughed. He said: "We'll have to slow down a bit." And he did.

The dream rolled on again. We passed under a second bridge
with the tugboat bowing down like a salute, passed all the houses I
had lived in. From so many of these windows I had looked with envy
and sadness at the flowing river and passing barges. Today I was free,
and traveling with my bed and my books. I was dreaming and flowing along with the river, pouring water out with pails, but this was a
dream and I was free.

Now it was raining. I smelled the captain's lunch and I picked
up a banana. The captain shouted: "Go on deck and say where it is
you want to stop."

I sat on deck under an umbrella, eating the banana, and watching the course of the voyage. We were out of Paris, in that part of the
Seine where the Parisians swim and canoe. We were traveling past
the Bois de Boulogne, through the exclusive region where only the
small yachts were allowed to anchor. We passed another bridge, and

reached a factory section. Discarded barges were lying on the edge of the water. The boat yard was an old barge surrounded with rotting skeletons of barges, piles of wood, rusty anchors, and pierced water tanks. One barge was turned upside down, and the windows hung half wrenched on the side.

We were towed alongside and told to tie up against the guardian barge, that the old man and woman would watch mine until the boss came to see what repairing had to be done.

My Noah's Ark had arrived safely, but I felt as if I were bringing an old horse to the slaughterhouse.

The old man and woman who were the keepers of this cemetery had turned their cabin into a complete concierge's lodge to remind themselves of their ancient bourgeois splendor: an oil lamp, a tile stove, elaborate sideboards, lace on the back of the chairs, fringes and tassels on the curtains, a Swiss clock, many photographs, bric-a-brac, all the tokens of their former life on earth.

Every now and then the police came to see if the roof was done. The truth was that the more pieces of tin and wood the boss nailed to the roof, the more the rain came in. It fell on my dresses and trickled into my shoes and books. The policeman was invited to witness this because he suspected the length of my stay.

Meanwhile the King of England had returned home, but no law was made to permit our return. The one-eyed man made a daring entry back and was expelled the very next day. The fat painter returned to his spot before the Gare d'Orsay—his brother was a deputy.

So passed the barge into exile.

The Mouse

The Mouse and I lived on a houseboat anchored near Notre Dame where the Seine curved endlessly like veins around the island heart of Paris.

The Mouse was a small woman with thin legs, big breasts, and frightened eyes. She moved furtively, taking care of the houseboat, sometimes silently, sometimes singing a little fragment of a song. Seven little notes from some folk song of Brittany, always followed by the clashes of pots and pans. She was always beginning the song and never ending it, as if it were stolen from the severity of the world and something frightened her, some fear of punishment or danger. Her room was the smallest cabin on the houseboat. The bed filled it, leaving only a corner for a little night table, and a hook for her everyday clothes, for her mouse-colored bedroom slippers, her mouse-colored sweater and skirt. Her Sunday clothes she kept under the bed in a box, wrapped with tissue paper. Her one new hat and a small piece of mouse fur were also kept in tissue paper. On the night table there was a photograph of her future husband, in a soldier's uniform.

Her greatest fear was of going to the fountain after dark. The houseboat was tied near the bridge and the fountain was under the bridge. It was there the hoboes washed themselves and slept at night. Or they sat in circles talking and smoking. During the day the Mouse fetched water in a pail, and the hoboes helped her to carry it in exchange for a piece of cheese, left-over wine, or a piece of soap. She laughed and talked with them. But as soon as night came she feared them.

The Mouse emerged from her little cabin all dressed in her mouse costume, a mouse-colored sweater, skirt and apron. She wore soft gray bedroom slippers. She was always scurrying along as if she were threatened. If she was caught eating, she lowered her eyes and sought to cover the plate. If she was seen coming out of her cabin she immediately concealed what she was carrying as if she were thieving. No gentleness could cross the border of the Mouse's fear, which was ingrained in the very skin of her thin legs. Her shoulders sloped as if too heavily burdened, every sound was an alarm to her ear.

I wanted to dispel her fear. I talked to her about her home, her family, the places where she had worked before. The Mouse answered me evasively, as if she were being questioned by a detective. Before every act of friendliness she was suspicious, uneasy. When she broke a dish she lamented: "Madame will take it out of my salary." When I assured her that I did not believe in doing this because it was an accident and an accident could happen equally to me, she was silent.

Then the Mouse received a letter which made her cry. I questioned her. She said: "My mother wants a loan of my savings. As I am saving to get married. I will lose the interest on the money." I offered to lend her the sum. The Mouse accepted but looked perplexed.

When she thought herself alone on the houseboat, the Mouse was happy. She sang her little beginning of a song she never finished. Sometimes instead of mending stockings she sewed for herself, for her marriage.

The first storm was caused by eggs. The Mouse was always given the same food as I ate, and not treated like a French servant. The Mouse was happy to have everything to eat, until one day when I ran short of money and I said to her: "Today just get some eggs and we'll make an omelet." The Mouse stood there, with a great fright in her eyes. She said nothing but she did not move. She was very pale, and then she began to cry. I put my hand on her shoulder and asked her what was the matter.

"Oh, Madame," said the Mouse, "I knew it could not last. We've had meat every day, and I was so happy, I thought at last I had found a good place. And now you are acting just like the others. Eggs. I can't eat eggs."

"But if you don't like eggs you can get something else. I don't mind. I only mentioned eggs because I was short of money today."

"It isn't that I don't like them. I always liked them, at home, on the farm. We ate a lot of eggs. But when I first came to Paris the lady I worked for was so stingy—you can't imagine what she was like. She kept all the closets under lock and key, she weighed the provisions, she counted the pieces of sugar I ate. She always scolded me for eating too much. She made me buy meat for her every day, but for me it was always eggs, eggs for lunch, dinner, every day, until I got deathly sick. And today when you said . . . I thought it was beginning all over again."

"You ought to know by now that I don't want you to be unhappy here."

"I'm not unhappy, Madame. I'm very happy here, only I didn't believe it. I thought all the time there must be a catch in it, or that you were only engaging me for a month and were intending to throw me out just before the summer vacation so that you would not have to pay my vacation, and I would be left stranded in Paris in the summer when there are no jobs to be had, or I thought you would send me off before Christmas so as not to have to give me a New Year's present, because all this happened to me before. I was in a house once where I could never go out; in the evenings I had to watch over the child, and on Sundays when they all went out I had to watch the house." She stopped. That was all she said for many weeks. She never referred to the eggs again. She seemed a little less afraid, but she scurried and hustled just as much, and ate as if she were ashamed to be caught eating. And again I could not cross the frontier of the Mouse's fear. Not even when I gave her half of my lottery ticket, not even when I gave her a frame for the photograph of her future husband, not even when I gave her writing paper the very day I caught her stealing mine.

Then one day I left the barge for a week, and the Mouse was left alone to guard it. When I returned I found it harder to catch the

Mouse's eyes, or to make her laugh. A woman who had been walking along the Quays with her lover lost her hat. It fell into the river. She knocked at our door and asked the Mouse if she could come onto the barge and try to catch it with a pole. It was floating around the other side. Everybody tried to reach it through the windows. The Mouse almost fell out carried down by the weight of the broom and the pull of the current. Everybody laughed, and the Mouse too. Then she got frightened hearing herself laugh, and she hurried away to her work.

A month passed. One day the Mouse was grinding coffee in the kitchen when I heard her groan. I found the Mouse very white, doubling up with pains in her stomach. I helped her to her cabin. The Mouse said it was indigestion. But the pains grew worse. She groaned for an hour, and finally asked me if I would get a doctor she knew about who lived very near. It was the doctor's wife who received me. The doctor had taken care of the Mouse before, but not since she lived on a houseboat. That made it impossible for the doctor to go and see her because he was a *grand blessé de guerre* and on account of his wooden leg he could not be expected to walk across an unsteady gangplank into a dancing houseboat. That was impossible, the wife repeated. But I pleaded with her. I explained that the gangplank was steady, that it had a railing on one side, that the houseboat never moved unless another barge was passing by, that it was anchored near the stairway and easy to get into. The river was very calm that day, and no accident was to be feared. The doctor's wife was half convinced and gave me a half promise that the doctor would come in an hour.

We watched for him out of the window, and we saw him arrive limping at the gangplank and hesitating in front of it. I walked over it to show him how steady it was, and he limped across it slowly repeating: "I am a *grand blessé de guerre*. I can't be taking care of people who live on houseboats." But he did not fall into the river. He entered the little cabin.

The Mouse was forced to make certain explanations. She was afraid she was pregnant. She had tried using something her sister had told her about, pure ammonia it was and now the pains were terrible.

The doctor shook his head. The Mouse had to uncover herself. Strange to see the little Mouse with her thin legs raised.

I asked her why she had not told me.

"I was afraid Madame would throw me out."

"On the contrary, I would have helped you."

The Mouse groaned. The doctor said: "You risked a terrible infection. If it does not come out now you'll have to go to the hospital."

"Oh, no, I can't do that, my sister will find out about it, and she'll be furious with me, and she will tell my mother."

"Maybe it'll come out all by itself but that is all I can do: I can't be mixed up in things like this. In my profession I must be careful, for my own sake. Bring me water and a towel."

He washed his hands carefully, talking all the time about the fact that he could not come back, and that all he hoped was that she would not have an infection. The Mouse was hunched in the corner of her bed looking anxiously at the doctor who was washing his hands of all responsibility. The *grand blessé de guerre* did not look at the Mouse as if she were a human being. Everything about him said clearly: you are only a servant, just a little servant, and like all of them you get into trouble, and it's your own fault. Now he said aloud: "All you servants make trouble for us doctors."

After washing his hands he limped down the gangplank with a definite good-by, and I returned to the cabin and sat on the Mouse's bed.

"You should have confided in me, I would have helped you. Lie quiet now, I'll take care of you."

"Don't send me to the hospital, my mother will find out. It only happened because you went away, and during those nights alone I was terribly afraid. I was so afraid of the men under the bridge that I let my young man stay here, and that's how it happened, because I was afraid."

That's how it happened to the Mouse, just in panic, she scurried into the trap, and was caught. That was the love the Mouse knew, this moment of fear, in the dark.

"To tell you the truth, Madame, it isn't worth it. I don't see anything to it at all. To have all this trouble afterwards, to get caught like this, and what for? It isn't anything extraordinary."

"Lie quiet, I'll come back later and see if you have a fever."

A few hours later the Mouse called me: "It happened, Madame, it happened!"

But the Mouse had a fever and it was mounting. There was an infection, and no doctor would come to the houseboat. As soon as they heard what it was about they refused to come. Especially for a servant. That happened too often. They must learn, they said, not to get into trouble.

I promised the Mouse to talk to her sister and invent some reason for her going away if she would let me take her to the hospital. She agreed and I offered to pack her valise. At the mention of valise the Mouse grew very pale. She lay inert and looked more frightened than ever. But I took her valise from under the bed and laid it beside her.

"Tell me where your clothes are. You will need soap, a toothbrush, a towel . . . "

"Madame . . ." The Mouse hesitated. She opened the small night table beside her. She handed out to me all the objects I had thought lost during the last month, my own soap, toothbrush, towel, one of my handkerchiefs, one of my powder puffs. So many things that I smiled. Out of the shelf came one of my chemises. I pretended not to notice. The Mouse's cheeks were red with fever. She packed her little valise carefully. She packed writing paper for her young man, and her knitting. She asked me to look for a book she wanted included. It was a Child's Reader. The Mouse had worn down the first ten pages, the stories of the lamb, the cow, the horse. She must have been reading the same pages for many years, they were so threadbare and gray like her bedroom slippers. I told the Mouse I would get her a new pair of slippers. The Mouse reached for her pocketbook which was hidden under the mattress.

"My God, has nobody ever given you anything?"

"No, Madame."

"If I were poor and sick in bed, wouldn't you give me a pair of slippers if I needed them?"

This idea frightened the Mouse more than any other. It was impossible for her to imagine this reversal.

"It isn't the same thing," said the Mouse.

She was carried out of the houseboat. She looked very small. She insisted on wearing a hat, her Sunday hat taken out of its tomb of tissue paper, and the very small fur neckpiece the color of her mouse eyes.

At the hospital they refused to take her in.

Who was the doctor taking care of her? None. Was she married? No. Who performed the abortion? Herself. This they doubted. They advised us to try another hospital. The Mouse was losing blood. The fever was consuming her. I took her to another hospital where they sat her on a bench. The Mouse kept a firm grasp on her little valise. They plied her with questions. Where did she come from? Where was the first place she worked in? The Mouse answered meekly. And after that? She could not remember the address. This held up the questionnaire for ten minutes. And before that? The Mouse answered again. She kept one hand over her stomach.

"This woman is losing blood," I protested, "are all these questions necessary?"

Well, if she didn't remember the third address, did she remember where she worked after that? And how long? The time was always two years. *Why?* asked the man at the desk. As if her not having stayed in the house longer were surprising, suspicious. As if she were the culprit.

"You performed the abortion perhaps?" asked the man turning to me.

The woman bleeding there on the bench meant nothing to them. The little round moist eyes, the tiny worn piece of fur around her neck, the panic in her. The brand-new Sunday hat and the torn valise with a string for a handle. The oily pocketbook, and the soldier's letters pressed between the leaves of a Child's Reader. Even this pregnancy, accomplished in the dark, out of fear. A gesture of panic, that of a mouse falling into a trap.

Under a Glass Bell

It was a stately house where many lives had accumulated and left their essences. It had the perfume of rich lives, of heavily impregnated furniture, and the very folds of the curtains contained secrets and sighs. It was also a house that seemed about to vanish. The tip of the labyrinthian stairway leading to the gate lost itself among the potted plants, the turrets dissolved into the overhanging branches of old trees. The glass doors and windows opened without sound, the floors were so highly polished they looked transparent. The ceilings were powdered white, the damask curtains were stiff like mummy costumes. The butlers knew about the fragility: they walked almost invisibly, seemingly not touching anything. What they carried back and forth was borne on silver trays with a minuet lightness of step and was to be received with equal delicacy. Wood, silk, and paint had the brittleness of preserved flowers. The curves of the legs of the chairs were full of debonair assertion like those of the ancient men of the family in their white stockings. The lace covers on the backs of the chairs were starched to look like paper and the paper flowers were painted to look like lace. The mirrors were framed with white roses made of sea shells. From the ceiling hung enormous glass chandeliers, blue icicle bushes shedding teardrops of blue glass light on the gold furniture.

On the mantelpiece, the shepherdesses, the angels, the gods and goddesses of porcelain, all seemed to have been caught while in motion by a secret enchantment and put to sleep with a dust of white sleep like those secret enchantments of nature enclosing the drops of water in dark caves and turning them into stalactite torches, candlesticks, hooded figures. That delicacy of design only created in a void, in great silence and great immobility. No violence here, no tears, no great suffering, no shouting, no destruction, no anarchy. The secret silences, the muted pains brought about by great riches, a conspiracy of tranquillity to preserve this flowerlike fragility in crystal, wood, and damask. The violins were muted, the hands were gloved, carpets were unrolled forever under the feet, and the gardens cottoned the sound from the world.

The light from the icicle bushes threw a patina over all objects, and turned them into bouquets of still flowers kept under a glass bell. The glass bell covered the flowers, the chairs, the whole room, the panoplied beds, the statues, the butlers, all the people living in the house. The glass bell covered the entire house.

Every day the silence, the peace, the softness, carved with greater delicacy the glass chandeliers, the furniture, the statuettes and laces, then covered them with glass. Under the giant glass bell the colors looked inaccessible, the shapes strongly beautiful as of something that can never be repeated. Everything had the transparency, the fragility of stalactite created in silence and obscurity and breaking when the caves are opened and the breath of man enters.

Jeanne was sitting with her two brothers in the room they used as children. They were sitting in front of an armored fireplace, in three children's chairs.

Her face seemed stemless and drooped listlessly as she monologued endlessly: 'Jean, Paul and I . . . nothing exists beyond our alliance. My own children do not mean as much to me as my brothers. I am devoted to my children only because I have given my word, I owe them that, but what I do for my brothers is a great joy. We cannot live without each other. If I am sick they get sick, if they are sick I get sick. All joys and anxieties are tripled. Their opinion of me and mine of them is our only standard. It forces us into a kind of heroic living. If I should ever say to Jean: 'You have done a petty thing,' he would kill himself. We three belong to the Middle Ages.

We have this need of heroism, and there is no place for such feelings in modern life. That is our tragedy. Once I wanted to be a saint. It seemed the only absolute act left to do, for what is most powerful in me is the craving for purity, greatness. I am not living on earth. Neither are my brothers. We are dead. We reached such heights in love that it made us want to die altogether with the loved one, and so we died. We are living in another world. Our having bodies is a farce, an anachronism. We were never even born. We have no ordi-nary sensual life, no contact with reality. My marriage was a farce, my brothers' marriages meaningless. When my children were born I didn't suffer. The births were difficult. I refused to take gas. I was amused. I wanted to see myself bringing children into the world. I worked hard. I felt pain, of course, but I didn't suffer like a human being. I felt pain detachedly, as if it were not happening to my body: I have no body. I have an external envelope which deludes others into thinking I am alive. My brothers and I hate to see each other. What we like is to have long conversations together from room to room, doors open, but not seeing each other. It enrages us to meet and kiss each other in that stupid, ordinary human way, to keep up the great farce of human movements, gestures, etc. when we are dead. And complete death would be so enjoyable, because everything we do together is an enjoyment. I can't bear to see them as bodies, to see them growing old. Once I sat writing letters and the two of them were playing cards. I looked at them and thought what a crime it was our being alive: it was a simulacrum, everything was really finished long ago. We have lived already, we are far away from husbands, wives, and children. I have tried so hard to love others, and I can up to a certain point, and then no further. Beyond that I begin to hate. Not one of us has any human sympathy. Jean does not understand why his wife weeps sometimes. We laugh at her. She is small and human. She weeps and we despise her for it. We never weep. The only thing I feel sometimes is fear, a terrific fear which catches me unaware sometimes like a fit of madness. Sometimes I become deaf in the street. I see automobiles passing and I hear nothing. At other times I seem to go blind. Everything becomes nebulous around me. But that only happens when I am alone. When I am alone I think

I go a little mad. Sometimes I say to my husband: 'Do you know, I believe I am supremely intelligent.' He says: 'How vain you are!' But it isn't vanity. It's an intelligence you get when you are dead. Sometimes while he is reading his newspaper I say: 'Wouldn't you like to be an archangel as I am?' He answers me: 'You're a child.' My brothers never say such things. We can describe to each other how it feels to be an archangel. Then when we are finished with that mood my brothers say: 'Let's pass to a new form of exercise.' I am a descendant of Joan of Arc. Only I have no role to play. I have nothing to save. We still sleep in the beds we used as children. My mother was the true Queen of France, she was loved by all the great men of her time. She ruled them. She never took care of us like a mother. She was always in the center of a great passion. She never kept a love, only while it was a passion. When the passions were over and she lost her beauty she took drugs. She lay all day in her canopied bed, her eyes burning, murmuring broken phrases. She shut her windows and lived by the light of night candles. Her eyes were dilated and saw nothing but her dreams. She ordered a dinner for twenty-five persons and then forgot about it and took a stronger dose of drugs. When I came home the chef and the housekeeper were running through the corridors shouting: 'Madame is raving about Napoleon. What are we going to do with the two dozen lobsters, the kilos and kilos of fruit? What shall we do? Madame is saying: "Bonjour, Napoleon, I must make a speech, and I don't know what to say."' I made the wrong start in life."

A Georgian Prince fell in love with Jeanne, and she tried to love him. But she complained that he uttered such ordinary words, that he could never say the magic phrase which would open her being.

It was Christmas morning and she went out with the Christmas tinsel rolled around her neck, carrying one of the glass birds perched on her little finger. She took a taxi to visit the Prince. When the taxi driver saw her he would not accept payment for the journey. He was a Russian. He may have remembered the Persian prints of a woman carrying a bird on her finger. He would not let Jeanne pay. He may have divined she was going to see the Prince. Jeanne put the tinsel around the taxi driver's neck and sat the bird on the taximeter, smiled and said: "Drive me home, please!"

That night I mailed Jeanne the first Persian print representing the Queen of Bijabur riding on a white steed harnessed with black velvet. It was handed to her on a silver tray with her breakfast. She thought it came from the Prince and again she took a taxi and this time she rang his bell and paid him a visit.

The next day she received a picture of Baz Bakadur and Rupmati riding together by moonlight. She thought the Prince could not articulate his dreams but that he could dream. She paid him another visit.

I sent her a print of Radha waiting for her lover Krishna. That evening they had supper together and, in accordance with the custom of his country, after they had eaten together they threw all the dishes out of the window.

The fourth day I sent her a Lover's Message in a Persian Garden filled with feather flowers. The fifth day I sent her the Prince and Princess riding through a mountainous region, a servant bearing a torch.

Before I exhausted my collection of Persian prints, Jeanne had discovered that Prince Mahreb could not dream at all, and again her face fell listlessly like a stemless plant.

In the garden one afternoon Paul fell asleep and as the sun was setting it projected the outline of his face on the back of the chair. Jeanne came up and kissed this shadow. Among shadows she was at ease.

The enormous house stood behind them, with a thousand eyes looking down at them.

Jeanne walked into the house and entered the room of mirrors. Ceilings of mirrors, floors of mirrors, windows of quicksilver opening on windows of quicksilver. The air was made of gelatine. Around her hair there was a saffron aureole, and her skin was a sea shell, an egg shell. There was a lunar wax light on the rim of her shoulder. Woman imprisoned in the stillness of mirrors washed only by jellied colors.

On her breast grew flowers of dust and no wind came from the earth to disturb them. Flowers of dust hung serenely. Around her waist a crinoline without its cover of lace and satin, a round crinoline like a bird cage. On her throat a brooch without stones, with its little silver hooks clutching emptiness. The fan in her hand was laceless and featherless, open and bare like winter branches. She breathed on the mirror. The dew of her breath on the mirror vanished. The mirror held nothing. She closed her eyes so many times: a tunnel of eyes closing. Countless sulphurous profiles touching each other accompanied by a rim of light. Countless women smiling; four women walking towards four women walking towards four women vanishing. She looked into the mirror until the dew of her anxiety clouded her face.

She wanted to be where she could not see herself. She wanted to be where everything did not happen twice. She walked, following the deep caverns of diminishing light. She touched ice and was bruised. To watch she must pause, and so what she caught was never the truth—the woman panting, dancing, weeping—it was only the woman who paused. The mirror was always one breath too late to catch the breathing.

Quickly, more quickly she turned to catch the face of her soul, but even when she moved at dream speed she saw the face of the actress, the small curtain closing inside of the pupil. She wanted to smash the mirror and be one. There was a joy of unveiling from which no human joy could call one back, there was joy without feet or voice or warmth, but the mirror revealed only the prying. If she could not catch the ultimate flame of life could she detect death? She bowed nearer to catch the immobility, the death. But the caverns within the pupil of the eye diminish and close at the sight of death. The eye dead could not see the eye dead in the mirror. At death all mirrors are covered, to bury reflection. Death never permitted an echo, death cannot be made visible, or cast the shadow of its presence.

She watched her sorrow. She looked at the tears. The sorrow unveiled and reflected before her ceased to be her own. It was the sorrow of another, with a space between them. She looked at the tears and they froze and died.

She ran out into the somnambulistic garden. Her brother was still asleep like one enchanted. The glass bell which separated them from the world was visible in the light. Would Jeanne see it? Would she smash it and be free? She did not see it. She kissed the shadow of her brother. He awakened. She said: "Let me touch something warm. Save me from reflections. The mirror frightened me."

But her hand was lying on the shadow of her brother and not on him. Then she said: "I am afraid that of the three of us I will be the first one to die. I am the lightest. I saw in the mirror, not my death but the image of myself in the tomb. I was wearing a brooch without stones, a crinoline with all its silk covering eaten away."

Her guitar was lying at her feet. As she said this the string broke.

The Mohican

He looked like a white Indian. He believed himself the last of the Mohicans, a faded, high-cheeked Indian transplanted from lost continents, whitened by long research in the Bibliothèque Nationale where he studied esoteric writings. He had a slow walk like a somnambulist enmeshed in the past and unable to walk into the present. He was so loaded with memories, cast down by them. Out of all his researches, his calculations, he extracted nothing but the poison of fatality. He saw only the madness of the world, the approach of a great world-engulfing catastrophe. For the Mohican all life was a minor crystal phenomenon on the surface of a planet. As a result people appeared to him without their human density. He saw their phosphorescence. He spoke of the intensity or feebleness of the light in them. Their angers were tongues of red hydrogen leaping out, an act of tenderness spewn forth from Venus. The fixity of his hypnotic glance discovered the water vapors of unsaid words, unmaterialized intentions. He saw us all without center of gravity, mere cosmic rays of light liberated by the explosion of unsteady stars.

At night he was preoccupied with the fear of what might happen if the sun burst. He awakened in the morning to remember the star that burst 1300 years ago. But his clairvoyance took him nowhere. His feet were encased in boots of lead. The core of him was like the core of earth, rock and iron unmelted by raging fire.

This fatalistic man, emerging from the depths of his past with intolerably open eyes, offered the world first of all an appearance of legendary elegance. His coat was handed to you with the care of a man who refused to be weighed by a speck of dust. This coat was hung preciously so that no wrinkle would form on it. His white collar was incredibly starchy, his cuffs dazzlingly white. His buff gloves had never been worn. His clothes showed no trace of having been lived in. Somnambulists made so few gestures, never knocked against objects, never fell. The trance carried him through all obstacles with an economy of gesture and the dream interposed itself between him and all he wanted to touch and feel. He himself passed invisibly, untouched, unattainable, giving at no time any proof of reality: no stain, tear, sign of wear and death coming. It seemed rather as if death had already passed, that he had died already to all the friction and usage of life, been pompously buried with all his possessions, dressed in his finest clothes, and was now walking through the city merely to warn us of the disruption of Europe.

He had the armature of the aristocrat, this strong armature which not only upheld his clothes but which forbade him to complain, to beg, to loosen or slacken either physically or spiritually, that extraordinary armature which was the only redeeming characteristic of nobility, the very last of the erect and stylized attitudes vanishing out of our world.

His voice too came from a great distance as he told about the auction sale of all his belongings, about the rapaciousness of the people fighting over his drawings, of how they bartered over intimate souvenirs, trophies, symbols, magic gifts, tokens of love. This spectacle and the loss of all the objects he loved hurt him so much that he felt calcined like those trees one sees sometimes in the south, still standing but with their entrails burnt to ashes. "Perhaps," said the Mohican, "all those who try to unveil the mysteries always have tragic lives. At the end they are always punished."

His talk was spherical, making enormous ellipses, catching the Turkish bath in Algeria where the beautiful boy massaged him so effectively that the Mohican had to run away from him—the Mohican's whole face expressing that he had not run away, a reminiscent mockery of the experience, something like the criminal's desire to return to the scene. If I pressed him I might discover that he had seen the boy again, but I would never know more than that. Yet while the Mohican talked, his very way of standing, of placing his weight upon one foot, of crossing his arms like a woman to protect the middle of his body, the trellis of shadows tabooing the middle of the body, while the eyes acknowledged perversity, everything helped one to imagine the Mohican and the boy together.

The Mohican always talked like a peeper, with imprecisions and a mysterious excitement due to what was passing through his memory at the moment and not at all to what he was saying. But the quick knowing ah! he uttered at the least indication of an adventure was so expressive that one felt the Mohican knew all there was to know or experience.

At the same time I suspected that it was the dilation of the incident through his imagination which created the feeling. Every scene he touched was immediately inflated, and the implications of mystery, terror, and perversity were so strong that the incident itself was drowned in them.

His talk was like the enormous wheel at the Fair, carrying little cages filled with people, the slow motion of the wheel, the little cages traveling spherically and the illusion of a vast circular voyage which never took one any nearer to the hub. One was picked up on the edge of the wheel, whirled in space, and deposited again without for an instant feeling nearer to its pulse. He carried people up and around him always at the same mathematical distance, breaking all the laws of human life which demand collisions and intermarriages.

He lived at the top of a hill overlooking Paris, near the white Sacre Coeur which made of it an Arabian island. He lived under the roof of a very small hotel, where the ceiling inclined over his bed. He gave to his room the order and barrenness of a monastic cell. He covered his books with cellophane. The blotter on his desk was white and spotless. On the walls hung horoscopes designed with geometric finesse. The planets in finely drawn lines of blue and red and black, traversing the "houses." The oppositions between them outlined in red ink, the squares in black, the conjunctions in blue.

The Moon and the Sun sometimes collided and fused in the struggle for domination. The ruler of the underworld, Pluto, had only
recently been discovered and the Mohican was frightened of it. So
frightened that he let me read the little red book which described its
significance and manner of operating, but would not tell any of us
how it might affect us directly and personally. He uttered unfinished
phrases about its great malefic power, the duality and the darkness
and the confusion it brought.

It was Pluto who sundered our being in two and left us hanging
on the finest thread between sanity and insanity. It made actors of us.
It doomed our loves.

Being driven always by a great desire for the ultimate revelations,
his secretiveness baffled me and I wanted to open Pandora's box. So
every time I came to see him it was the first question I put to him,
and each time he edged sideways, with an oblique glance, and said:
"It is too soon to say definitely what it does to us."

The Mohican sat in his little room under the roof, and from
there he watched over all our lives and made predictions. All he
needed were the hour, date and place of birth. Then he would vanish for several days into his laboratory of the soul, and we would
only see him again when the horoscope was, as he said, properly
infused, as if he were making some herb potion for us. Did he really
know when disease and madness would strike? Did he know when
we were going to love, unite, separate? The Mohican believed that he
knew, and when we were lost or confused we wanted to believe too.
What we discovered with time was that he knew no more than we
did about the actuality of an event. He could not distinguish between
potentiality and fulfillment, between the dream and the actuality. Many experiences and events which he predicted never came to
the surface of our life, they only happened in the dream. And many
dreams which he expected to remain as myths, took a human form
and became actual.

His greatest suffering came from his incapacity to interpret his
own horoscope. Because the ultimate statement depended on the in-
terpretation of the facts he could not trust his objectivity. He was
absolutely crushed by a sense of fatality.

When the war came he was sitting in the Bibliothèque Nationale doing research work on mythology. Gradually the books he was reading were removed to safer places. The Mohican found himself deprived of sustenance. He studied whatever was left: crystallography, herbs and perfumes, witchcrafts and alchemy. But soon they too were packed in cellars, in Pluto's underworlds. This meant spiritual starvation and the Mohican lost weight.

When the Germans came, because of his charts, maps, calculations, and predictions of the death of Hitler, he was arrested as a celestial saboteur.

Je suis le plus malade des Surréalistes

It was Savonarola looking at me, as he looked in Florence in the Middle Ages while his followers burned erotic books and paintings on an immense pyre of religious scorn. It was the same drawn childish mouth of the monk, the deep-set eyes of the man living in the caverns of his separation from the world. Between us there was this holocaust burning, in his eyes the inquisitor's condemnation of all pleasure.

"You want to burn me, your eyes condemn me," I said.

"You are Beatrice Cenci. Your eyes are too large for a human being."

He was sitting in a deep chair in the corner of the room, his angular body struggling against the softness of the chair, looking for stones, stones to match the leanness and hardness of his bones, the petrified tautness of his nerves. Sweat was pouring from his brow. He did not wipe it off. He was sitting taut, with his vision burning in the pupil of his eye, and the intensity of the man who committed suicide every moment, but unwilling to die alone, and bringing all others down with him into his death. Unwilling to die alone, and with his eyes murdering and condemning those who did not want to die, insulting those who smiled, moved away from death.

There was a door at his right. He leaped away from my eyes and walked into the hothouse. I thought he was moved by his secret pain to vanish from us and I did not expect him to return. When he reappeared there was the scum of veronal on his lips, and his gestures were slower.

"I am starting a Theater of Cruelty. I am against the objectivity of the theater. The drama should not take place on a stage separated from the audience, but right in the center of it, so near to them that they will feel it happening inside of themselves. The place will be round like an arena, the people sitting close to the actors. There will be no talking. Gestures, cries, music. I want scenes like the ancient rituals, which will transport people with ecstasy and terror. I want to enact such violence and cruelty that people will feel the blood in them. I want them to be so affected that they will participate. They will cry out and shout and feel with me, with all of us, the actors."

This explosion, this shattering of the being into ecstasy and terror was what Pierre wanted to accomplish with his Theater of Cruelty.

And I wanted to follow him. With all the fervor of my eyes I said to him I would follow him into all his inventions and creations.

Nobody would follow him. When he stood up and shouted about his theater, they laughed. They laughed because each cell of the dream that Pierre projected was enormous, swollen out of the blood and the sea in his blood, the water of his body, his sweat and tears, his passion for the absolute. No one else believed in the absolute, no one else dared to explode to reach ecstasy. No one followed him. They laughed.

From the crystal cell in which his dream had placed me, his words, I could see his tiny figure wanting by tautness and intensity to dominate this world. I no longer heard the laughter. We were together inside of the sphere of his dream of the theater and his dilated vision had encircled me, enchanted me.

We walked out together, out of the hall where the laughter had wounded him. We walked until we reached the outer walls of the city. A drunkard was asleep on the mud. A hungry dog was prowling. The dog began to dig into the earth, swiftly, nervously, until he dug a hole. Pierre watched him with a shudder of fear. I saw him break into perspiration, as if he were making the effort at the digging. The gaunt dog made a deep hole in the ground. Pierre watched him and then he cried: "Stop him! He is making a tunnel. I will be caught inside of it and suffocate to death. Stop him! I can't breathe."

I shouted at the dog who cowered away. But the hole was there and Pierre looked at it as if it were going to swallow him.

"People say that I am mad," he said.

"You are not mad, Pierre, I see all you see, I feel all you feel. You are not mad."

We turned away from the hole. We walked in the darkness. Pierre added to the long tunnel of his own thoughts which I could feel in the night, and they were thoughts of mistrust, mistrust of me. Every moment what I expected was the Savonarola who would explode in condemnation of me, for all that I had betrayed in my quest of the dream. He walked at my side like a severe confessor to whom I had confessed nothing because he would forgive nothing. But it was not Savonarola who appeared. It was Heliogabalus.

Pierre led me to the Louvre Museum, where the paintings and statues were illuminated by spotlights, and stopped before the statue of Heliogabalus.

"Do you see the resemblance?" he asked me.

In the face of stone I saw the face of Pierre. I saw the face of Pierre when he retired behind life, behind the flesh world, into the mineral, everything drawn inward and petrified. I saw the face of Pierre in which nothing moved except the eyes, and the eyes moved like a terrified ocean, seeking wildly to withdraw also, but unable to, still liquid, still foaming and smoking, and this effort of the water in his body against the invasion and petrification of the stone, made the bitter sweat break out all over his body.

In the face of stone I saw the face of the Theater of Cruelty. Without the liquid eyes still weeping in Pierre's face, I saw the grimace of cruelty deeply etched in the jaw. The mouth was no longer a mouth but an open cavern in which took place great human sacrifices.

Pierre stood there and his eyes ceased to move in their orbit. They were equally transfixed. His voice began to unroll down the corridors of statues: "Your senses are affected by a statue. In you the body and spirit are tremendously bound together, but it is the spirit that must win. I feel in you a world of unborn feelings and I will be the exorcist to awaken them. You yourself are not aware of all of them. You are calling to be awakened with all your female senses which in you are also spirit. Being what you are, you must understand what a painful joy I feel at having discovered you. Destiny has granted me more than I ever dreamed of demanding. And like all things brought by destiny it came in a fatal way, without hesitation, so beautiful that it terrifies me. My own spirit and life are made up of illuminations and eclipses which play constantly inside of me and therefore around me and on everything that I love. For those who love me I will always be a source of deep sorrow. You already observed that at times I have intuitions, swift divinations, and at other times I am absolutely blind. The simplest thing eludes me then, and you will need all the subtle understanding you have to accept this mixture of darkness and light."

As I did not answer he added: "I love your silences, they are like mine. You are the only being before whom I am not distressed by my own silences. You have a vehement silence, one feels it is charged with essences, it is a strangely alive silence, like a trap open over a well, from which one can hear the secret murmur of the earth itself."

His eyes were blue with languor, and then would turn black with pain and rebellion. He was a knot of tangled nerves vibrating in all directions without a core of peace.

"I feel this moving silence of yours speaking to me and it makes me want to weep with joy. You inhabit a different domain than mine, you are my complement. If it is true that our imaginations love the same images, desire the same forms, physically and organically you are warmth whereas I am cold. You are supple, languorous, whereas I am unyielding. I am calcined. I am like a mineral. What I fear most is that I may lose you during one of those periods when half of me is cut off from the other. What a divine joy it would be to possess a being like you who are so evanescent, so elusive."

"Brother, brother," I wanted to say, "you are confusing the nature of our love for each other."

"You will never follow me into destruction, into death."

"I will follow you anywhere."

"With you I might return from the abysms in which I have lived. I have struggled to reveal the workings of the soul behind life, its deaths. I have only transcribed abortions. I am myself an absolute abysm. I can only imagine myself as a being phosphorescent from all its encounters with darkness. I am the one who has felt most deeply the stutterings of the tongue in its relation to thought. I am the one who has best caught its slipperiness, the corners of the lost. I am the one who has reached states one never dares to name, states of soul of the damned. I have known those abortions of the spirit, the aware-ness of the failures, the knowledge of the times when the spirit falls into darkness, is lost. These have been the daily bread of my days, my constant obsessional quest for the irretrievable."

Before the eyelids came down, the pupils of the eyes swam up-ward and I could see only the whites. The eyelids fell on the white and I wondered where his eyes had gone. I feared that when he opened them again the sockets would be empty like those of Helio-gabalus' statue.

He stood firm, like silex, nobly, proudly, a sudden lightning joy in the eyes when I said: "I will follow you wherever you want. I love the pain in you. There are worlds deeper down, each time we sink and are destroyed, there are deeper worlds beneath which we only reach by dying."

His gestures were slow, heavy, like a hypnotist. He did not touch me. His hands merely hovered over me, over my shoulder, heavy with a magnetic weight, despotic, like a command. I had come dressed in black, red and steel, with a steel bracelet and necklace, dressed as a warrior not to be touched by Pierre. I felt his desire oppressive, taut, obsessive. I felt his presence growing more powerful, huge, all iron and white flames.

"All the beauty I thought lost in the world is in you and around you. When I am near you I no longer feel my being contracting and shriveling. This terrible fatigue which consumes me is lifted. This fatigue I feel when I am not with you is so enormous that it is like what God must have felt at the beginning of the world, seeing all the world uncreated, formless, and calling to be created. I feel a fatigue of the tongue seeking to utter impossible things until it twists itself into a knot and chokes me. I feel a fatigue at this mass of nerves seek-ing to uphold a world that is falling apart. I feel a fatigue at feeling, at the fervor of my dreams, the fever of my thought, the intensity of my hallucinations. A fatigue at the sufferings of others and my own. I feel my own blood thundering inside of me, I feel the horror of falling into abysms. But you and I would always fall together and I would not be afraid. We would fall into abysms, but you would carry your phosphorescences to the very bottom of the abysms. We could fall together and ascend together, far into space. I was always exhausted by my dreams, not because of the dreams, but because of the fear of not being able to return. I do not need to return. I will find you everywhere. You alone can go wherever I go, into the same mysterious regions. You too know the language of the nerves, and the perceptions of the nerves. You will always know what I am saying even if I do not."

I looked at his mouth whose edges were blackened with lau-danum. Would I be drawn towards death, towards insanity? To be touched by Pierre meant to be poisoned by the poison which was destroying him. With his hands he was imprisoning my dreams be-cause they were like his, he was laying heavy hands on me.

"You did not respond to my touch," he accused me. "You have become cold and distant. You are dangerous and I always knew it. I was deceived by your glidingness, your alertness, your vibrancy. You are the plumed serpent, snake and bird together, you look like spirit and yet I thought you were warm and soft. You glide with your body close to the earth, and you wear your plume high in the air too, walk-ing over the earth and through the air at the same time, waving this tiny blue plume in the air, in the dream."

"Brother, brother," I said. "I have such a deep love for you, but do not touch me. I am not to be touched. You are the poet, you walk inside my dreams, I love the pain and the flame in you, but do not touch me."

❖ ❖ ❖ ❖

He was brought in a strait jacket and the doctor was smiling at the puzzled way he looked down at his crossed arms and his bound legs.

"Why are you so violent? Why are you afraid of coming here?"

"You are going to take my strength away, you had everything ready to take my strength away."

"Why should I want to take your strength away?"

"Because of the white phoenix who is born every hundred years. The white phoenix is a friend of the good. And the man with the white tie who warned me of the danger he was of the order of the white phoenix who is born every hundred years and is a friend of the good. The white phoenix is now inside of me and the black eagles are envious, they are the friends of evil and they are against me. They come, six of them, in gray suits, and they pursue me. I see them sometimes in a coach, that is when it is a long time ago in a print I saw, of course today they come in an automobile. The President died today, or else I would not have been brought here."

"The President did not die today," said the doctor.

"Not he, perhaps, but then the other, the one who is like him."

"There is one like him?"

"Yes, just as there is one who is exactly like me, who thinks everything I think, it is a woman, it is my betrothed, but I can't find her."

"Does she know you are here?"

"Not yet."

"Who else goes after you?"

"A monk who is castrated and who sometimes takes the form of a woman."

"Where do you see this personage?"

"In the mirror."

"What else do you see in the mirror?"

"The monk who is castrated and takes the form of a woman."

"You know I don't wish you any wrong, don't you?"

"Yes, yes, I know that you have everything ready to take my strength away like Abelard."

"Why should I want to take your strength away?"

"Because I desired my betrothed, the woman who thinks as I do."

"How often do you see the white phoenix?"

"It is born only once in a hundred years so you see there are many more black eagles than there are white phoenixes, and so the good is always persecuted and followed by six men dressed in gray in a coach as in a print I saw, or if you prefer, in an automobile as it would be today."

"You tried to commit suicide, didn't you?"

"Yes, because nobody loved me. I was sent to live the life of Musset and as you know he suffered a great deal and nobody loved him, and as you know he drank a great deal because nobody loved him. I was sent to live the life of Musset and to explain the prophecy he made in a café before he was hanged."

"He was hanged?"

"Nobody knows that and I came to save his honor."

"How can you save his honor?"

"By explaining the prophecy he made in the café before it was closed which I got from him as I stood in front of the mirror waving a white rag at the sound of the angelus."

"The angelus?"

"I was born at noon when the angelus was ringing. White is the color of the white phoenix and the black eagles think they are superior to him, they think they have all the power, but this power is in me now, and that is why you want to take my strength away."

"Was that why you got violent when I wanted to bring you here?"

"No, that time it was merely to show off, because I know that you expected me to, you were expecting it so I did it, because I know all that I tell you you think it comes out of a detective story, and you know that it is true that I have read one hundred thousand novels."

"Why did you want to die?"

"I have the blue love, because the woman who was in every way reciprocal to all that I thought did not love me, so I threw myself into the Nile in Egypt. I have many enemies."

"Why?"

"Because when one is white like the white phoenix and the others are black one has enemies. It is always the same. It is the white phoenix that you want to take away from me."

The doctor bade him good-by, and told him that he could leave the room. The madman got up. The two aides stood near him. They knew that his feet were bound and that he could not walk without help, but they looked at him and made no movement towards him.

They let him take two steps on his way out of the room. The doctor let him take two steps with his bound feet and smiled at the way he was tangled and bound. The madman took two steps and fell. He was permitted to fall.

Ragtime

The city was asleep on its right side and shaking with violent nightmares. Long puffs of snoring came out of the chimneys. Its feet were sticking out because the clouds did not cover it altogether. There was a hole in them and the white feathers were falling out. The city had untied all the bridges like so many buttons to feel at ease. Wherever there was a lamplight the city scratched itself until it went out.

Trees, houses, telegraph poles, lay on their side. The ragpicker walked among the roots, the cellars, the breathing sewers, the open pipe works, looking for odds and ends, for remnants, for rags, broken bottles, paper, tin and old bread. The ragpicker walked in and out of the pockets of the sleeping city with his ragpicker's pick. In and out of the pockets over the watch chain on its belly, in and out of the sleeves, around its dusty collar, through the wands of its hair, picking the broken strands. The broken strands to repair mandolins. The fringe on the sleeve, the crumbs of bread, the broken watch face, the grains of tobacco, the subway ticket, the string, the stamp. The ragpicker worked in silence among the stains and smells.

His bag was swelling.

The city turned slowly on its left side, but the eyes of the houses remained closed, and the bridges unclasped. The ragpicker worked in silence and never looked at anything that was whole. His eyes sought the broken, the worn, the faded, the fragmented. A complete object made him sad. What could one do with a complete object? Put it in a museum. Not touch it. But a torn paper, a shoelace without its double, a cup without saucer, that was stirring. They could be transformed, melted into something else. A twisted piece of pipe. Wonderful, this basket without a handle. Wonderful, this bottle without a stopper. Wonderful, the box without a key. Wonderful, half a dress, the ribbon off a hat, a fan with a feather missing. Wonderful, the camera plate without the camera, the lone bicycle wheel, half a phonograph disk. Fragments, incompleted worlds, rags, detritus, the end of objects, and the beginning of transmutations.

The ragpicker shook his head with pleasure. He had found an object without a name. It shone. It was round. It was inexplicable. The ragpicker was happy. He would stop searching. The city would be waking up with the smell of bread. His bag was full. There were even fleas in it, pirouetting. The tail of a dead cat for luck.

His shadow walked after him, bent, twice as long. The bag on the shadow was the hump of a camel. The beard the camel's muzzle. The camel's walk, up and down the sand dunes. The camel's walk, up and down. I sat on the camel's hump.

It took me to the edge of the city. No trees. No bridge. No pavement. Earth. Plain earth trodden dead. Shacks of smoke-stained wood from demolished buildings. Between the shacks gypsy carts. Between the shacks and the carts a path so narrow that one must walk Indian file. Around the shacks palisades. Inside the shack rags. Rags for beds. Rags for chairs. Rags for tables. On the rags men, women, brats. Inside the women more brats. Fleas. Elbows resting on an old shoe. Head resting on a stuffed deer whose eyes hung loose on a string. The ragpicker gives the woman the object without a name. The woman picks it up and looks at the blank disk, then behind it. She hears tick, tick, tick, tick, tick. She says it is a clock. The ragpicker puts it to his ear and agrees it ticks like a clock but since its face is blank they will never know the time. Tick, tick, tick, the beat of time and no hour showing.

The tip of the shack is pointed like an Arab tent. The windows oblique like oriental eyes. On the sill a flower pot. Flowers made of beads and iron stems, which fell from a tomb. The woman waters them and the stems are rusty.

The brats sitting in the mud are trying to make an old shoe float like a boat. The woman cuts her thread with half a scissor. The ragpicker reads the newspaper with broken specs. The children go to the fountain with leaky pails. When they come back the pails are empty. The ragpickers crouch around the contents of their bags. Nails fall out. A roof tile. A signpost with letters missing.

Out of the gypsy cart behind them comes a torso. A torso on stilts, with his head twisted to one side. What had he done with his legs and arms? Were they under the pile of rags? Had he been thrown out of a window? A fragment of a man found at dawn.

Through the cracks in the shacks came the strum of a mandolin with one string.

The ragpicker looks at me with his one leaking eye. I pick a basket without bottom. The rim of a hat. The lining of a coat. Touch myself. Am I complete? Arms? Legs? Hair? Eyes? Where is the sole of my foot? I take off my shoe to see, to feel. Laugh. Glued to my sole is a blue rag. Ragged but blue like cobalt dust.

The rain falls. I pick up the skeleton of an umbrella. Sit on a hill of corks perfumed by the smell of wine. A ragpicker passes, the handle of a knife in his hand. With it he points to a path of dead oysters. At the end of the path is my blue dress. I had wept over its death. I had danced in it when I was seventeen, danced until it fell into pieces. I try to put it on and come out the other side. I cannot stay inside of it. Here I am, and there the dress, and I forever out of the blue dress I had loved, and I dance right through air, and fall on the floor because one of my heels came off, the heel I lost on a rainy night walking up a hill kissing my loved one deliriously.

Where are all the other things, I say, where are all the things I thought dead?

The ragpicker gave me a wisdom tooth, and my long hair which I had cut off. Then he sinks into a pile of rags and when I try to pick him up I find a scarecrow in my hands with sleeves full of straw and a high top hat with a bullet hole through it.

The ragpickers are sitting around a fire made of broken shutters, window frames, artificial beards, chestnuts, horse's tails, last year's holy palm leaves. The cripple sits on the stump of his torso, with his stilts beside him. Out of the shacks and the gypsy carts come the women and the brats.

Can't one throw anything away forever? I asked.

The ragpicker laughs out of the corner of his mouth, half a laugh, a fragment of a laugh, and they all begin to sing.

First came the breath of garlic which they hang like little red Chinese lanterns in their shacks, the breath of garlic followed by a serpentine song:

Nothing is lost but it changes
into the new string old string
in the new bag old bag
in the new pan old tin
in the new shoe old leather
in the new silk old hair
in the new hat old straw
in the new man the child
and the new not new
the new not new
the new not new

All night the ragpicker sang the new not new the new not new until I fell asleep and they picked me up and put me in a bag.

The Labyrinth

I was eleven years old when I walked into the labyrinth of my diary. I carried it in a little basket and climbed the moldy steps of a Spanish garden and came upon boxed streets in neat order in a backyard of a house in New York. I walked protected by dark green shadows and followed a design I was sure to remember. I wanted to remember in order to be able to return. As I walked, I walked with the desire to see all things twice so as to find my way back into them again. The bushes were soft hairy elbows touching mine, the branches swords over my head. They led me. I did not count the turns, the chess moves, the meditated displacements, the obsessional repetitions. The repetitions prevented me from counting the hours and the steps. The obsessions became the infinite. I was lost. I only stopped because of the clock pointing to anguish. An anguish about returning, and about seeing these things but once. There was a definite feeling that their meaning could only be revealed the second time. If I were forced to go on, unknowing, blind, everything would be lost. I was infinitely far from my first steps. I did not know exactly why I must return. I did not know that at the end I would not find myself where I started. The beginning and the end were different, and why should the coming to an end annihilate the beginning? And why should the beginning be retained? I did not know, but for the anguish in my being, an anguish over something lost. The darkness before me was darker than the darkness behind me.

Everything was so much the same and equal before and around me that I was not certain I had turned sufficiently in the path to be actually walking towards the place from which I started. The clouds were the same, the croaking of the frogs, the soft rain sound of fountains, and the immobile green flame of evergreens in boxes. I was walking on a carpet of pages without number. Why had I not numbered the pages? Because I was aware of what I had left out; so much was left out that I had intended to insert, and numbering was impossible, for numbering would mean I had said everything. I was walking up a stairway of words. The words repeated themselves. I was walking on the word pity pity pity pity pity pity. My step covered the whole word each time, but then I saw I was not walking. When the word was the same, it did not move, nor did my feet. The word died. And the anguish came, about the death of this word, about the death of the feeling inside of this word. The landscape did not change, the walk was without corners; the paths so mysteriously enchained I never knew when I had turned to the right or left. I was walking on the word obsession with naked feet: the trees seemed to press closer together, and breathing was difficult. I was seeking the month, the year, the hour, which might have helped me to return. In front of me was a tunnel of darkness which sucked me violently ahead, while the anguish pulled me backwards. The escalator of words ran swiftly under me, like a river. I was walking on my rebellions, stones exploding under my feet. Following the direction of their heaviest fragment might take me back. Yet all the time I knew that what I would find would be white bleached bones, sand, ashes, decomposed smiles, eyes full of holes like cooled lava.

My feet were slipping on accumulated tears like the slippery silt of river banks, on stones washed by slow waters. I touched rock-crystal walls with white foaming crevices, white sponges of secret sorrows set in a lace of plant skeletons. Leaves, skins, flesh had been sucked of their juices, and the juices and sap drunk by the crevices, flowing together through the river bed of stillborn desires.

Legs and arms and ears of wax were hung as offerings, yielded to the appetite of the cave, nailed with humble prayers for protection that the demon might not devour those who passed.

I walked pinned to a spider web of fantasies spun during the night, obstinately followed during the day. This spider web was broken by a foghorn, and by the chiming of the hours. I found myself traversing gangways, moats, gangplanks while still tied to the heaving, straining cord of a departing ship. I was suspended between earth and sea, between earth and planets. Traversing them in haste, with anguish for the shadow left behind, the foot's imprint, the echo. All cords easily untied but the one binding me to what I loved.

I sank into a labyrinth of silence. My feet were covered with fur, my hand with leather, my legs wrapped in accordion-pleated cotton, tied with silken whips. Reindeer fur on my breast. Voicelessness. I knew that like the reindeer even if the knife were thrust into me at this moment, I would not even sigh.

Fragments of the dream exploded during my passage through the moats, fell like cutting pieces from dead planets without cutting through the fur and cotton of this silence. The flesh and fur walls breathed and drops of white blood fell with the sound of a heartbeat. I did not want to advance into the silence, feeling I might lose my voice forever. I moved my lips to remember the words I had formed, but I felt they no longer articulated words. My lips moved like the sea anemone, with infinite slowness, opening and closing, rolling under the exterior pressure, to breathe, forming nothing but a design in water. Or they moved like the noses of animals quivering at the passing wind, to detect, to feel, forming no word but recognition of an odor. Or they moved as flowers close for the night, or against the invasion of an insect. They breathed with fin slowness, with the cadence of a bulb flowering.

I was not moving any more with my feet. The cave was no longer an endless route opening before me. It was a wooden, fur-lined crib, swinging. When I ceased stepping firmly, counting my steps, when I ceased feeling the walls around me with fingers twisted like roots, seeking nourishment, the labyrinthian walk became enlarged, the silence became airy, the fur disintegrated, and I walked into a white city.

It was a honeycomb of ivory-white cells, streets like ribbons of old ermine. The stone and mortar were mixed with sunlight, with musk and white cotton. I passed by streets of peace lying entangled like cotton spools, serpentines of walls without doorways, veiled faces and veiled windows ascending, dissolving into terraces, courtyards, emptying into the river. I heard secret fountains of laughter, hooded voices. I heard the evening prayer like a lament spilling on shining mosaics and the veins of the cobblestones under my feet were like a chaplet between monk's fingers. I passed windowless houses erupting at the tip in flowered terraces, a Vesuvius of flowers. And now I was inside the soft turning canals of a giant ear, inside the leaves of intricate flowers, streets spiraling like sea shells, lost in a point, and the bodies passing me were wrapped in cotton capes, and breathed into each other's faces. In their hands the sand of time was passing slowly. They carried enormous rusty keys to open the gates which divided the city. The palm leaves were waving, gently content, and the city lay like a carpet under contemplative feet. I was awakened by a sound of paper unrolling. My feet were treading paper. They were the streets of my own diary, crossed with bars of black notes. Serpentines of walls without doorways, desires without issues. I was lost in the labyrinth of my confessions, among the veiled faces of my acts unveiled only in the diary. I heard the evening prayer, the cry of solitude recurring every night. My feet touched the leaves of intricate flowers shriveling, paper flowers veined with the nerves of instruments. Enormous rusty keys opened each volume, and the figures passed armless, headless, mutilated. The white orifice of the endless cave opened. On the rim of it stood a girl eleven years old carrying the diary in a little basket.

Through the Streets of My Own Labyrinth

Landing at Cadiz I saw the same meager palm trees I had carefully observed when I was eleven years old and passing through on my way to America. I saw the Cathedral I had described minutely in my diary, I saw the city in which women do not go out very much; the city I said I would never live in because I liked independence. When I landed in Cadiz I found the palm trees, the Cathedral, but not the child I was.

The last vestiges of my past were lost in the ancient city of Fez, which was so much like my own life, with its tortuous streets, its silences, secrecies, its labyrinths and its covered faces.

In the city of Fez I became aware that the little demon which devoured me for twenty years, the little demon which I fought for twenty years, had ceased eating me.

I was at peace walking through the streets of Fez, absorbed by a world outside of myself, by a past which was no longer my past, by sicknesses one could touch and name and see, visible sicknesses, leprosy and syphilis.

I walked with the Arabs, chanted and prayed with them to a god who ordained acceptance. I shared their resignation.

With them I crouched in stillness, lost myself in streets without issues—the streets of my desires; forgot where I was going, to sit by the mud-colored walls listening to the copper workers hammering copper trays, watching the dyers dipping their silk in rainbow-colored pails.

Through the streets of my own labyrinth I walked in peace at last, strength and weakness welded in the Arab eyes by the dream. The blunders I made lay like the refuse on the doorsteps and nourished the flies. The places I did not reach were forgotten because the Arab on his donkey or on naked feet walked forever between the walls of Fez as I shall walk forever between the walls and fortresses of my diary. The failures were inscriptions on the walls, half effaced by time, and with the Arabs I let the ashes fall, the old flesh die, the inscriptions crumble. I let the cypresses alone watch the dead in their tombs, I let the madnesses be tied in chains as they tie their madmen. I walk with them to the cemetery not to weep, but carrying colored rugs and bird cages for a feast of talk with friends—so little does death matter, or disease, or tomorrow. The Arabs dream, crouching, fall asleep chanting, beg, pray, with never a cry of rebellion; night watchmen, sleeping on the doorsteps in their soiled burnooses; little donkeys bleeding from maltreatment. Pain is nothing, pain is nothing here; in mud and hunger, everything is dreamed. The little donkey—my diary burdened with my past—with small faltering steps is walking to the market. . . .

The All-Seeing

When I rang his bell I could hear the parting of the beaded curtains of his room, and I knew he could see me through a little glass
eye in his door through which I could not see him. Through this
glass eye the hallway appeared immeasurably long and the person
standing before the door many miles away and small, but extraordinarily distinct like a personage out of the past seen through the
telescope of memory on a day of clear visibility.

As he appeared in the dark hallway he illumined it with his
eyes, his own eyes like the aurora borealis, a waving of luminous
chiffon, such an immense and deep phenomenon of light like the eye
of the universe.

At first a blue softness, like a melting of snow and light, then
lightning which revealed lucidity, and then a transparency like a dawn
opening the worlds of divination. His gaze came from the remotest
worlds of light and silence, piercing through our exterior, exposing
instantly the naked soul and remained there before the exposure, full
of surprise and wonder and awe.

They had in them the roving gaze of the mariner who never
attaches himself to what he sees, whose very glance is roving, floating, sailing on, and who looks at every person and object with a sense
of the enormous space around them, with a sense of the distance
one can put between one's self and one's desires, the sense of the

enormousness of the world, and of the tides and currents that carry us onward.

Women were at times deceived by the hunger in them. The hunger and avidity of them, they believed he wanted them, and gave themselves, and found this hunger unchanged, and the distance increased; his eyes seemed as horizonless as the ocean itself, as unfixable, as mutable and unconquerable.

Over the absorbing glance that could drink and never be satisfied fell gentle eyelids of the most delicate skin, and in the gentle way they fell there was goodness. In the length and softness of his blond eyelashes there was a silken yieldingness, but over the delicate eyelids fell savage eyebrows, wild like a bushman's. The small nose was vulnerable and pure, the brow spiritual, the mouth full and sensual, and the hands those of a peasant asserting his strength. Such as he stood there, he was constantly in mutation between fierceness and yielding, between assertiveness and sudden eclipses of his whole being which caused him to pale and vanish before certain people who were not of his climate. Constantly oscillating even in the same moment between a physical appetite which his mouth demanded and some secret flame of a dream sapping at his strength.

He was never dressed, but costumed to suit some mood of a new self. He was in disguise. Whether he wore the black flowing tie of the romantic bohemian, the cap of the apache, the coat of a horse-racing man, the black striped pants of a provincial bourgeois, the bow tie of the second-rate actor, or the bull-red scarf of the professional pickpocket, one knew he would only appear once in this role.

His room was like an explorer's den, a lair of furs, the cave of a magician. The color of blood predominated. There were furs on the bed, rugs on the walls. In one corner stood a blue sled like a small bark sailing heavenward towards the planets. Inside the sled a reindeer fur. Hung on the walls, reindeer boots and gloves. The boots with their curled toes did not point earthward but airily out towards adventures and difficulties. Inside the sled a small lamp shed a blue Nordic light.

A violin hung on the wall.

His violin nailed to the wall and never touched since the day his mother had said to him: "So you failed to get the prize you struggled for? You're hurt, you're humiliated, but I'm happy. Now you will stop playing the violin and wasting your life. You will be a man like your father, not a fiddler. I'm very glad you did not win the prize. You would have gone to Paris to study and become a good-for-nothing. We never had musicians in our family."

With one phrase she had destroyed his first passion. He hung his violin on a wall. The strings snapped gradually and hung dead.

Seeking this that he had lost without knowing it, he became restless and a rover, a prober, he became the archeologist of his own soul, he searched and wandered looking blindly for the source of that music killed by the mother. He was possessed with restlessness, timelessness, forgetfulness. He lived in a labyrinth and a haze. He feared to look backward and seeing the shadow of this that had been killed in him but he also feared to stay where he was and lose it alto-gether. So he pursued it blindly to the farthest corners of the world, returning each time to the violin which hung on his wall crucified and muted.

The music that was in him was never silenced, it flooded his place and every object vibrated with it. Wherever he went the place was filled with resonances like the inside of an instrument. The har-monies of his being lay concealed in the very shell of his misery as the echo of the sea inside the sea shells, and while he talked about the loss of his violin, the loss of music, one could place one's ear against any object in his room, against his walls, against his rugs, against his pillows, and hear distinctly the music his mother had not been able to kill.

Each time that he embarked on a new transformation, or dis-guise, or voyage, he was driven not by pleasure or curiosity, but by the sight of the crucified violin. It wounded him, to see the broken strings. So he rushed again into multiple changes, to return loaded with new objects like votive offerings to the violin. He brought the entire universe back into his room: spoons from Mount Athos carved like chalices with inlaid silver, a mushroom shaped like a holy water stand—a holy water stand of poison, erotic post cards from China, skeletons from the caves of the Canary Islands, beer glasses from Munich and rosaries from Lourdes, dried mint from

India, water from the Black Sea in a bottle, Chinese manuscripts and the skeleton of a bird from Tahiti, the magic plunders and chaos of the cave of Ali Baba.

To catch him at the moment of departure it was clear from his haste and anguish that it was a wound driving him, the pain of his silenced hands aching for the bow and strings, the shaft of the violin bow which had entered his soul like a splinter.

Just before he talked he seemed like a very soft animal, sensitive and porous, just before he talked, when his malady was not perceptible. He seemed pregnable and without taint, sailing freely like a ship without moorings.

It was only when he began to talk that one saw how chained he was to his obsessions. Every step he took was marked by a gasp of anguish. Only while actually in movement was he lulled.

No sooner had the marvelous befallen him than he grasped it with his peasant hands with the violence of a man who was not certain of having seen it, lived it, and who wanted to reassure himself of its palpability. Everything which befell him would be ripped apart, analyzed, commented. As if he felt that behind all his possessions, some diabolical substitution was being offered him, as if he knew that what he desired did not lie in all the treasures that might be offered him.

By moving, escaping, and distilling for himself only the essences and the legends (he turned every woman into a mirage) he did not reach the freedom and the ecstasy he sought, but anguish, an abysmal anguish. After he pursued so ardently only the atmosphere of the dream, and by prestidigitations, transformed everything into a mirage, then he lamented the absence of warmth and humanity. The further he cut himself from the ugly, the sordid, the animal, from sickness which he overlooked, from poverty which he disregarded, from his body which he maltreated, from human ties he would not submit to, from protection which he disdained, the more anguish he felt.

The dream did not give him contentment.

He was lonely.

So he fell in love with the Unknown Woman of the Seine, who had drowned herself many years ago and who was so beautiful that at the Morgue they had made a plaster cast of her face. It was this picture he carried about. Around her he embroidered the most luxurious enchantments which she could not destroy, as other women destroyed the enchantments he cast around them. Her silence permitted the unfolding of all his inventions. In death alone could love grow to such an absolute. One of the lovers must be dead for the absolute to flourish, this impossible, unattainable flower of the infinite. In death alone there is no betrayal and no loss. So Jean gave his infinite love to the drowned Unknown Woman of the Seine. His spiritually autocratic love found no rival in death.

But he was lonely.

We locked ourselves inside his dream, with the objects he had chosen, and first there was contentment like a drug, enveloping and dissolving. While he talked the Chinese gong knocked against our senses, evoking Tibetan deserts and ceremonies. On the piano navigated a small African pirogue with four wooden Africans silhouetted against the light. The deer horns protruded from the walls holding open erotic books traversed by a knife. Two hunters' knives were crossed over our head. Delicate sea plants bloomed in unexpected places, starfishes were glued on the mirror and skeleton leaves on the windowpanes. The windowpanes were painted so that one could not see the street, and so the glance was thrown inwardly again into contemplation.

"When I went to Lapland," said Jean, holding an empty opium pipe, "I found the country of silence. People gathered together, sat in circles, smoking and smiling, but they do not talk. The reindeer has no voice with which to lament or cry. I looked everywhere for the secret of their speech and found it only in the trees. The trees talked for them. The trees had tortured arms, gaunt legs, the faces of totem poles. They talked and complained and sighed and threw imploring arms up towards the silence."

Essences and flavors began to fill the room. We sat on tiny children's chairs from Greece, before the fire. Jean caressed his empty opium pipe and said: "Do you think we will ever find our twin in love?"

"People who are twins," I said, "there is a curse upon their love. Love is made of differences and suffering and apartness, and of the

struggle to overcome this apartness. Two people who love the dream
above all else would soon both vanish altogether. One of them must
be on earth to hold the other down. And the pain of being held down
by the earth, reality, that is what our love for others will be."

"You know how I live, by what I call the alternating currents
Sometimes I am afraid to get cut off altogether. But when I do love,
what anxiety I feel, what doubts."

"Doubts not of love, but of reality. You live in a mirage and you
seek to be incarnated through the body of your love. With your gift
for metamorphosis you can remove yourself so far that in love you
seek the warmth and the reassurance of your very existence. You float
too easily, you are too easily cut off. Then when love holds you in
bondage for a moment you feel anguish. But at some time or other
you will have to accept having a body, a reality, being in bondage. You
will have to enter the prison of human life and accept the suffering."

At the word suffering he took his air of flight and departure. His
eyes alighted on the North Pole. Then his eyes returned and rested
on me, knowing from me no pain would strike at him. "Don't you
describe my transparence," he said, "because you yourself are like a
rainbow, an easily vanishing color. You only appear when the atmosphere is propitious. You can walk over the waters, you are so light.
Others will see you do it and they will want to follow you but they
will drown. You are also a mirror, a mirror in which people see themselves fulfilled, the free self. I see myself free when I look at you. You
are the perfect mirror without flaws which gives the reflection of the
future self. But will I be free before it is too late? I feel that other people are sewn together loosely, naturally, with a space in between the
stitches for breathing. I am sewn too tightly, with too many stitches
overlapping, so that I suffocate."

"Here we breathe freely."

"Yes, because in the maze of the dream we cannot see our
human sorrows."

Jean stood now before the blurred and covered window which
did not open into the street. He said: "I am behind the window of a
prison. I am a prisoner. There is always a window, and I am always
behind it, looking out, and desiring to escape to countries and places

which I imagine to be light, wall-less, illimitable. And you are a prisoner of another kind. You are barred behind your loves and your compassions. When the doors open, and you are on the verge of freedom, you take the fatal glance backward and see the one behind you who is not free and you retract your step and enchain yourself to this one while the prison doors close again. You are a voluntary prisoner who will not walk out *alone*. You are always preparing the flight for others. And so time passes."

"But of course, Jean, we have the dream, this drug given to prisoners of distinction."

The Eye's Journey

He worked on small canvases with a touch as light as a cobweb and coloring made of mirages. He lived there, at the bottom of the sea, but a bottom of the sea cluttered with objects from shipwrecks. Fishes passed through one-eyed towers, anchors, and weeds grew out of hulks. All that could fall from a ragpicker's bag lay heaving restlessly buried by Hans in a shipwreck of broken moods, lost fragments of irretrievable worlds. The green which enveloped the broken objects was the green of mildew, and the browns which shrouded the sceneries was the brown of stagnation.

Aware it was through the Eye that he had passed to reach this other side of the world, he always painted a small human eye in the corner, the secret door of his escape into the deep regions unknown to the surface of the eyes. He had traversed the Eye as through a looking-glass, into its roots, into the before-birth and after-death, and there found these layers of light, waves of wrecked moods, cells of immobility and pain corroded by the rust of stagnation.

A storm was perpetually suspended over this, a storm from no one knew where, so that the miracles of beauty stillborn in the water were constantly threatened by an impending lightning, near explosion. The small fixed eye in the corner of the painting was hypnotized with terror. A world about to vanish always, on the brink of absolute catastrophe.

At first when the day began, the passage through the Eye was made smoothly and Hans flowed out of his room and beyond his misery. His body was as still as if it had been anesthetized and the Eye alone carried him everywhere, swimming, sliding, dissolving, penetrating. But after a few hours the colors died on his finger tips, and the eye in the corner of the painting became glazed and then utterly blind. He never knew if it was his body awakening to the consuming hunger, or the coldness of the room which enshrouded him, or the gradual consciousness of the wall in front of his window, the wall of the Prison de la Sante, or the stains on his own four walls, or the limpness of his one suit hanging on a peg, the emptiness of his torn pockets, the dust on the panes, or the falsetto voice of the concierge. . . . But the Eye closed.

It was then he sailed out shiftily and insecurely, towards drink. In drink he might find again some of the lost warmth, the lost incan-descence, the lost dilation. As soon as he drank, the sky melted and the clouds galloped, the dampness ceased to gnaw and became like some gentle shower, and the cramp in his stomach from lack of food, dissolved. Warmth and color and dilation of the heart and bowels into an infinite world.

It was his room that was growing tighter around him, growing smaller, smaller, emptier, and the solitude would strangle him. Now everything was open, while the glass was full, but when the glass was empty and the bartender refused to fill it, then he fell into an abysm again, his legs weakened and his eyes blurred. He lost everything then, the world shrank again, and the solitude was deeper because now people were laughing at him, people were talking about him. The woman who took care of him at the Hospital was telling every-one the most intimate, revolting details of his illness, and they were laughing at him. The policeman knew he had not paid his rent for a year and was waiting to arrest him. He could not walk directly home either, he must catch it obliquely, tangentially: the friend, the glass of wine, home, they would all escape from his grasp if he reached for them directly. And while he stood there he knew there was someone searching his room and trying to steal his paintings, so in the end he ran back to his room and insulted the concierge with his eyes protruding with inordinate anger. She swore no one had been in his room, but he knew. He knew that he merely had not had the time to carry away the best of the paintings, but that he would return and that he must sit there and watch for the thief. So he refused to go out for his meals. The concierge was anxious about him and occasionally brought him a plate of soup, but he would not take it because it was poisoned.

Finally two strange men came to call for Hans. Hans knew why they came. They were going to keep him hidden until the Other could steal his paintings and then they would let him go free. There was no defense against them: he was too weak to fight them. He asked permission to dress himself.

He wondered whether he should go without shoes. He would rather save them for his return. They were so worn they would not last very long. What he most regretted was that now he would miss watching the big snake at the Zoo. Every day he had been there at feeding time because the big snake was fed live mice. He liked to watch the terror of the mouse who knew what awaited it as soon as it was placed in the cage. Its fixed terror, its incapacity to run away as soon as the snake began to gaze upon it with its unblinking stare. The snake knew it would not struggle but wait transfixed with terror. So the snake lingered and delayed the moment of devouring the mouse, enjoying the certainty. The mouse could not move, but its little eyes made a thousand revolutions of terror while the eyes of the snake remained round, unblinking.

Hans felt he was the mouse, and watched his own fate, every day, his own passivity. His own eyes bulged like those of a perpetually frightened man.

Even his paintings on the small canvases he made with the certainty that they were to be devoured. He had moments when he felt he was running a race with a giant snake: the more paintings he could weave out of himself as a cocoon weaving silk spools, the more he could delay the final annihilation.

Now while the men waited he hesitated in the middle of the room. And then he thought: "But suppose that I die? I can't be buried without shoes. I must put my shoes on. I may die. If they forbid me to paint I will die." And he laced his shoes on carefully, for his death.

Hans was permitted to paint in the cell room which was so much like the room he had been living in. But slowly, from the drinking, his eyesight began to fail him. They operated on them and saved one. For the lost one they gave him a glass eye. And now Hans knew that he was no longer the mouse but the snake. He was the one who watched everything and would begin to devour. Because his Eye was fixed on the world. He could no longer move back and forth through the Eye. When he saw flames leaping all around him he merely stared at the flames. He stared at the flames as they raged around him. When the fire was put out in the asylum he had lost his glass eye. He was neither mouse nor snake any longer.

The Child Born Out of the Fog

Walking towards the river, walking through circles of children playing, walking under the arch of loitering men's eyes, walking into torn newspapers petaling upward, walking over sliced tin cans, walking past broken windows (the stones are lying on bare floors), walking over charred doorways (the fire did not last long, there was not much to feed on), walking past meager grocery stores, sleepy bars, passing people with concave stomachs of hunger.

Ringing a bell to a little house where the bell hangs loose on a wire, the door slants askew, the hinges complain and the lock seems weak and removable.

But out of the curtainless window leans the long hair of a woman men will write poems for, the blue-green eyes of Undine after she had wept, the full creole mouth of southerners, the laughing, up-turned nose, a face of open tenderness throwing down the little street a soft welcome, a child's smile eclipsed by early sorrows.

There is a rustle inside, the rustle to prevent the guest of honor from stepping into intimate disorders. Someone has come and certain objects must be banished, and when the door is opened the secret disorder has ceased and one is allowed to step up the green stairway to a room of green walls, colored lamps, with books on the floor, records on the couch, a painted fireplace, into a sunburst of colors as on the Madagascar hats.

The windows giving on the street had been covered with triangles of colored paper and the room might have been in an Arabian city.

Sarah was sitting on a low chair. She had taken off her green sweater and she was mending a hole in it.

Don was strumming his guitar in readiness for his performance at the night club. Don's black hair was softly waved, his dark skin shed copper tones. His hands on the guitar were sensitive and slender.

He asked: "Has Pony had her dinner?"

And just then the little girl Pony entered sideways and one saw first of all her very round black eyes. Two tears had frozen on her cheeks, tears at having been deserted by both parents, but halfway down her face they had stopped flowing because she had found them again. Soft dark brown curls and two hands stretched towards the white mother and the dark father for equal consolation.

In Peru there is a song about God the Potter. God the Potter was baking men. He baked one lot and did not time it well, and when he took the tray out there were men with white hair, white eyelashes and dead-white skins, absolutely faded specimens. He laid them aside (they escaped to Norway). The second lot was a little better, but the third was perfect and that was the Indian. And surely Pony too had come out of the third lot baked à point.

The first lot had produced Sarah's first love, a blond boy who had not loved her deeply. "The sun used to bleach his hair to gold."

Everyone who is hurt takes a long voyage.

You travel as far as you can from the place of the hurt.

Sarah traveled far from gold hair to black hair as men of old traveled into virgin forests to heal a wound, as they traveled to foreign lands to forget a face.

She had traveled from a land of cold words to a land of warm words, from a land of detachment to a land of tenderness, from shallowness to richness. She had sailed from a port where a young man spoke words born on the edge of his handsome mouth to where words issued from the pit where Pony's tears came from when she was deserted.

Sarah had taken a long voyage, for she had much to forget—her mother's words: sensuality is a crime; and her father's words: the Negro is unclean.

She had walked through a park one summer evening with Don, with whom she had attended a political meeting, and listening to his words she heard the accents of truth, the accents of wholeness. The voice was rich because there was everything in it: blood and sinews, heart and warmth, joy and pain, body and heart pulsing together. Even his politeness came from the heart as he pushed away the branches from her face, as he talked of love and hatred, pure because they were either love or hatred, not composites, not half loves and half hatreds.

In this park, with a dense summer fog surrounding them, she heard the voice of Don and the voices of her feelings deep like a forest.

The fog isolated them but here was a world. The fog ostracized them: two lost beings, one lost in the pain of betrayal by one, the other in danger of death and ignominy and betrayal by all because he was born of the Potter's third lot.

At first they played a game like children, of losing and finding each other in the fog. One moment when he hid too well, and she could not catch the faintest rustle of his presence among the trees, she knew that if she did not find him again she would be alone.

And Pony was the little child who was born out of the fog.

When the fog lifted, when the day came, stones were thrown at them, and Don's life was in danger,—from the father, from strangers in the street, so they never walked together and she could not carry Pony safely through the streets.

The game begun in the park was prolonged forever into reality turned into a daily danger of loss.

Don would say every day: "It's time for me to leave."

Sarah would say: "Give me a little change for the bus."

Don would say: "I will meet you at the restaurant."

Would he see her? Would she find him? Would harm befall him?

They looked at each other as if the fog would fall again, as if one might get lost forever on the way.

He left the house with his guitar, walking proudly and not proud, walking nobly and smoothly, and yet hurt and bowed.

She sat in the bus alone.

At one moment the bus passed him.

They were not allowed to wave to each other.

Hejda

The unveiling of women is a delicate matter. It will not happen overnight. We are all afraid of what we shall find.

Hejda was, of course, born in the Orient. Before the unveiling she was living in an immense garden, a little city in itself, filled with many servants, many sisters and brothers, many relatives. From the roof of the house one could see all the people passing, vendors, beggars, Arabs going to the mosque.

Hejda was then a little primitive, whose greatest pleasure consisted in inserting her finger inside pregnant hens and breaking the eggs, or filling frogs with gasoline and setting a lighted match to them. She went about without underclothes in the house, without shoes, but once outside she was heavily veiled and there was no telling exactly the contours of her body, which were at an early age those of a full-blown woman, and there was no telling that her smile had that carnivorous air of smiles with large teeth.

In school she had a friend whose great sorrow was her dark color. The darkest skin in the many shaded nuances of the Arabian school. Hejda took her out into the farthest corner of the school garden one day and said to her: "I can make you white if you want me to. Do you trust me?"

"Of course I do."

Hejda brought out a piece of pumice stone. She very gently but very persistently began to pumice a piece of the girl's forehead. Only

66

when the pain became unendurable did she stop. But for a week, every day, she continued enlarging the circle of scraped, scarred skin, and took secret pleasure in the strange scene of the girl's constant lamentations of pain and her own obstinate scraping. Until they were both found out and punished.

At seventeen she left the Orient and the veils, but she retained an air of being veiled. With the most chic and trim French clothes, which molded her figure, she still conveyed the impression of restraint and no one could feel sure of having seen her neck, arms or legs. Even her evening dresses seemed to sheathe her. This feeling of secrecy, which recalled constantly the women of Arabia as they walked in their many yards of white cotton, rolled like silk around a spool, was due in great part to her inarticulateness. Her speech revealed and opened no doors. It was labyrinthian. She merely threw off enough words to invite one into the passageway but no sooner had one started to walk towards the unfinished phrase than one met an impasse, a curve, a barrier. She retreated behind half admissions, half promises, insinuations.

This covering of the body, which was like the covering of the spirit, had created an unshatterable timidity. It had the effect of concentrating the light, the intensity in the eyes. So that one saw Hejda as a mixture of elegance, cosmetics, aesthetic plumage, with only the eyes sending signals and messages. They pierced the European clothes with the stabbing brilliancy of those eyes in the Orient which to reach the man had to pierce through the heavy aura of yards of white cotton.

The passageways that led one to Hejda were as tortuous and intricate as the passageways in the oriental cities in which the pursued women lost themselves, but all through the vanishing, turning streets the eyes continued to signal to strangers like prisoners waving out of windows.

The desire to speak was there, after centuries of confinement and repression, the desire to be invaded and rescued from the secretiveness. The eyes were full of invitations, in great contradiction to the closed folds of the clothes, the many defenses of the silk around the neck, the sleeves around the arms.

Her language was veiled. She had no way to say: look at Hejda who is full of ideas. So she laid out cards and told fortunes like the women of the harem, or she ate sweets like a stunted woman who had been kept a child by close binding with yards of white cotton, as the feet of the Chinese women had been kept small by bandaging. All she could say was: I had a dream last night (because at breakfast time in the Orient, around the first cup of dark coffee, everyone told their dreams). Or she opened a book accidentally when in trouble and placed her finger on a phrase and decided on her next course of action by the words of this phrase. Or she cooked a dish as colorful as an oriental market place.

Her desire to be noticed was always manifested, as in the Orient, by a bit of plumage, a startling jewel, a spangle pasted on her forehead between the eyes (the third eye of the Oriental was a jewel, as if the secret life so long preserved from openness had acquired the fire of precious stones).

No one understood the signals: look at Hejda, the woman of the Orient who wants to be a woman of tomorrow. The plumage and the aesthetic adornment diverted them like decoration on a wall. She was always being thrust back into the harem, on a pillow.

She had arrived in Paris, with all her invisible veils. When she laughed she concealed her mouth as much as possible, because in her small round face the teeth were extraordinarily large. She concealed her voraciousness and her appetites. Her voice was made small, again as the Chinese make their feet small, small and infantile. Her poses were reluctant and reserved. The veil was not in her timidities, her fears, in her manner of dressing, which covered her throat and compressed her overflowing breasts. The veil was in her liking for flowers (which was racial), especially small roses and innocent asexual flowers, in complicated rituals of politeness (also traditional), but above all in evasiveness of speech.

She wanted to be a painter. She joined the Académie Julian. She painted painstakingly on small canvases—the colors of the Orient, a puerile Orient of small flowers, serpentines, confetti and candy colors, the colors of small shops with metallic lace-paper roses and butterflies.

In the same class there was a dark, silent, timid young Rouma-
nian. He had decadent, aristocratic hands, he never smiled, he never
talked. Those who approached him felt such a shriveling timidity in
him, such a retraction, that they remained at a distance.

The two timidities observed each other. The two silences, the
two withdrawals. Both were oriental interiors, without windows on
the external world, and all the greenery in the inner patio, all their
windows open on the inside of the house.

A certain Gallic playfulness presides in the painting class. The
atmosphere is physical, warm, gay. But the two of them remain in
their inner patio, listening to birds singing and fountains playing. He
thinks: how mysterious she is. And she thinks: how mysterious he is.

Finally one day, as she is leaving, he watches her repainting the
black line on the edge of her eyes out of a silver peacock. She nimbly
lifts up the head of the peacock and it is a little brush that makes
black lines around her oriental eyes.

This image confounds him, ensorcells him. The painter is
captivated, stirred. Some memory out of Persian legends now adorns
his concept of her.

They marry and take a very small apartment where the only
window gives on a garden.

At first they marry to hide together. In the dark caverns of their
whisperings, confidences, timidities, what they now elaborate is a
stalactitic world shut out from light and air. He initiates her into his
aesthetic values. They make love in the dark and in the daytime
make their place more beautiful and more refined.

In Molnar's hands she is being remolded, refashioned, stylized.
He cannot remold her body. He is critical of her heaviness. He dislikes
her breasts and will not let her ever show them. They overwhelm him.
He confesses he would like her better without them. This shrinks
her within herself and plants the seed of doubt of her feminine value.
With these words he has properly subjugated her, given her a doubt
which will keep her away from other men. He bound her femininity,
and it is now oppressed, bound, even ashamed of its vulgarity,
of its expansiveness. This is the reign of aesthetic value, stylization,
refinement, art, artifice. He has established his domination in this. At

every turn nature must be subjugated. Very soon, with his coldness, he represses her violence. Very soon he polishes her language, her manners, her impulses. He reduces and limits her hospitality, her friendliness, her desire for expansion.

It is her second veiling. It is the aesthetic veils of art and social graces. He designs her dresses. He molds her as far as he can into the stylized figures in his paintings. His women are transparent and lie in hammocks between heaven and earth. Hejda cannot reach this, but she can become an odalisque. She can acquire more silver peacocks, more poetic objects that will speak for her.

Her small canvases look childlike standing beside his. Slowly she becomes more absorbed in his painting than in her own. The flowers and gardens disappear.

He paints a world of stage settings, static ships, frozen trees, crystal fairs, the skeletons of pleasure and color, from which nature is entirely shut off. He proceeds to make Hejda one of the objects in this painting; her nature is more and more castrated by this abstraction of her, the obtrusive breasts more severely veiled. In his painting there is no motion, no nature, and certainly not the Hejda who liked to run about without underwear, to eat herbs and raw vegetables out of the garden.

Her breasts are the only intrusion in their exquisite life. Without them she could be the twin he wanted, and they could accomplish this strange marriage of his feminine qualities and her masculine ones. For it is already clear that he likes to be protected and she likes to protect, and that she has more power in facing the world of reality, more power to sell pictures, to interest the galleries in his work, more courage too. It is she who assumes the active role in contact with the world. Molnar can never earn a living, Hejda can. Molnar cannot give orders (except to her) and she can. Molnar cannot execute, realize, concretize as well as she can, for in execution and action she is not timid.

Finally it is Molnar who paints and draws and it is Hejda who goes out and sells his work.

Molnar grows more and more delicate, more vulnerable, and Hejda stronger. He is behind the scene, and she is in the foreground now.

He permits her love to flow all around him, sustain him, nourish him. In the dark he reconquers his leadership. And not by any sensual prodigality, but on the contrary, by a severe economy of pleasure. She is often left hungry. She never suspects for a moment that it is anything but economy and thinks a great abundance lies behind this aesthetic reserve. There is no delight or joy in their sensual contact. It is a creeping together into a womb.

Their life together is stilted, windowless, facing inward. But the plants and fountains of the patio are all artificial, ephemeral, immobile. A stage setting for a drama that never takes place. There are colonnades, friezes, backgrounds, plush drops but no drama takes place, no evolution, no sparks. His women's figures are always lying down, suspended in space.

But Hejda, Hejda feels compressed. She does not know why. She has never known anything but oppression. She has never been out of a small universe delimited by man. Yet something is expanding in her. A new Hejda is born out of the struggle with reality, to protect the weakness of Molnar. In the outer world she feels larger. When she returns home she feels she must shrink back into submission to Molnar's proportions. The outgoing rhythm must cease. Molnar's whole being is one total negation; negation and rejection of the world, of social life, of other human beings, of success, of movement, of motion, of curiosity, of adventure, of the unknown.

What is he defending, protecting? No consuming passion for one person, but perhaps a secret consuming. He admits no caresses, no invitations to love-making. It is always "no" to her hunger, "no" to her tenderness, "no" to the flow of life. They were close in fear and concealment, but they are not close in flow and development. Molnar is now frozen, fixed. There is no emotion to propel him. And when she seeks to propel him, substitute her élan for his static stagnation, all he can do is break this propeller.

"Your ambitions are vulgar."

(She does not know how to answer: my ambitions are merely the balance to your inertia.)

A part of her wants to expand. A part of her being wants to stay with Molnar. This conflict tears her asunder. The pulling and tearing bring on illness.

Hejda falls.

Hejda is ill.

She cannot move forward because Molnar is tied, and she cannot break with him.

Because he will not move, his being is stagnant and filled with
poison. He injects her every day with this poison.

She has taken his paintings into the real world, to sell, and in so
doing she has connected with that world and found it larger, freer.

Now he does not let her handle the painting. He even stops painting. Poverty sets in.

Perhaps Molnar will turn about now and protect her. It is the
dream of every maternal love: I have filled him with my strength. I
have nourished his painting. My painting has passed into his painting. I am broken and weak. Perhaps now he will be strong.

But not at all. Molnar watches her fall, lets her fall. He lets poverty install itself. He watches inertly the sale of their art possessions,
the trips to the pawnbroker. He leaves Hejda without care. His
passivity and inertia consume the whole house.

It is as if Hejda had been the glue that held the furniture together. Now it breaks. It is as if she had been the cleaning fluid and
now the curtains turn gray. The logs in the fireplace now smoke
and do not burn: was she the fire in the hearth too? Because she
lies ill objects grow rusty. The food turns sour. Even the artificial
flowers wilt. The paints dry on the palette. Was she the water, the
soap too? Was she the fountain, the visibility of the windows, the
gloss of the floors? The creditors buzz like locusts. Was she the
fetish of the house who kept them away? Was she the oxygen in
the house? Was she the salt now missing from the bread? Was she
the delicate feather duster dispelling the webs of decay? Was she
the silver polish?

Tired of waiting for her to get well—alone, he goes out.

✤ ✤ ✤ ✤

Hejda and Molnar are now separated. She is free. Several people help her to unwind the binding wrapped around her personality
first by the family life, then by the husband. Someone falls in love

with her ample breasts, and removes the taboo that Molnar had placed upon them. Hejda buys herself a sheer blouse which will reveal her possessions.

When a button falls off she does not sew it on again.

Then she also began to talk.

She talked about her childhood. The same story of going about without underwear as a child which she had told before with a giggle of confusion and as if saying: "what a little primitive I was," was now told with the oblique glance of the strip-teaser, with a slight arro-gance, the *agent provocateur* towards the men (for now exhibitionism placed the possibility in the present, not in the past).

She discards small canvases and buys very large ones. She paints larger roses, larger daisies, larger trellises, larger candied clouds, larger taffy seas. But just as the canvases grow larger without their con-tent growing more important, Hejda is swelling up without growing. There is more of her. Her voice grows louder, her language, freed of Molnar's decadent refinement, grows coarser. Her dresses grow shorter. Her blouses looser. There is more flesh around her small body but Molnar is not there to corset it. There is more food on her table. She no longer conceals her teeth. She becomes proud of her appetite. Liberty has filled her to overflowing with a confidence that everything that was once secret and bound was of immense value. Every puerile detail of her childhood, every card dealer's intuition, every dream, becomes magnified.

And the stature of Hejda cannot bear the weight of her ambi-tion. It is as if compression had swung her towards inflation. She is inflated physically and spiritually. And whoever dares to recall her to a sense of proportion, to a realization that there are perhaps other painters of value in the world, other women, becomes the traitor who must be banished instantly. On him she pours torrents of abuse like the abuse of the oriental gypsies to whom one has refused charity— curses and maledictions.

It is not desire or love she brings to the lovers: I have discovered that I am very gifted for love-making!

It is not creativity she brings to her painting: I will show Molnar that I was a better painter!

Her friendships with women are simply one long underground rivalry: to excel in startling dress or behavior. She enters a strained, intense competition. When everything fails she resorts to lifting her dress and arranging her garters.

Where are the veils and labyrinthian evasions?

She is back in the garden of her childhood, back to the native original Hejda, child of nature and succulence and sweets, of pillows and erotic literature.

The frogs leap away in fear of her again.

Birth

"The child," said the doctor, "is dead."

I lay stretched on a table. I had no place on which to rest my legs. I had to keep them raised. Two nurses leaned over me. In front of me stood the doctor with the face of a woman and eyes protruding with anger and fear. For two hours I had been making violent efforts. The child inside of me was six months old and yet it was too big for me. I was exhausted, the veins in me were swelling with the strain. I had pushed with my entire being. I had pushed as if I wanted this child out of my body and hurled into another world.

"Push, push with all your strength!"

Was I pushing with all my strength? All my strength?

No. A part of me did not want to push out the child. The doctor knew it. That is why he was angry, mysteriously angry. He knew. A part of me lay passive, did not want to push out anyone, not even this dead fragment of myself, out in the cold, outside of me. All in me which chose to keep, to lull, to embrace, to love, all in me which carried, preserved, and protected, all in me which imprisoned the whole world in its passionate tenderness, this part of me would not thrust out the child, even though it had died in me. Even though it threatened my life, I could not break, tear out, separate, surrender, open and dilate and yield up a fragment of a life like a fragment of the past, this part of me rebelled against pushing out the child, or anyone, out in the cold, to be picked up by strange hands, to be buried in strange places, to be lost, lost, lost. . . . He knew, the doctor. A few hours before he adored me, served me. Now he was angry. And I was angry with a black anger at this part of me which refused to push, to separate, to lose.

"Push! Push! Push with all your strength!"

I pushed with anger, with despair, with frenzy, with the feeling that I would die pushing, as one exhales the last breath, that I would push out everything inside of me, and my soul with all the blood around it, and the sinews with my heart inside of them, choked, and that my body itself would open and smoke would rise, and I would feel the ultimate incision of death.

The nurses leaned over me and they talked to each other while I rested. Then I pushed until I heard my bones cracking, until my veins swelled. I closed my eyes so hard I saw lightning and waves of red and purple. There was a stir in my ears, a beating as if the tympanum would burst. I closed my lips so tightly the blood was trickling. My legs felt enormously heavy, like marble columns, like immense marble columns crushing my body. I was pleading for someone to hold them. The nurse laid her knee on my stomach and shouted: "Push! Push! Push!" Her perspiration fell on me.

The doctor paced up and down angrily, impatiently. "We will be here all night. Three hours now. . . ."

The head was showing, but I had fainted. Everything was blue, then black. The instruments were gleaming before my eyes. Knives sharpened in my ears. Ice and silence. Then I heard voices, first talking too fast for me to understand. A curtain was parted, the voices still tripped over each other, falling fast like a waterfall, with sparks, and cutting into my ears. The table was rolling gently, rolling. The women were lying in the air. Heads. Heads hung where the enormous white bulbs of the lamps were hung. The doctor was still walking, the lamps moved, the heads came near, very near, and the words came more slowly.

They were laughing. One nurse was saying: "When I had my first child I was all ripped to pieces. I had to be sewn up again, and then I had another, and had to be sewn up, and then I had another. . . ."

The other nurse said: "Mine passed like an envelope through a letter box. But afterwards the bag would not come out. The bag would not come out. Out. Out. . . ." Why did they keep repeating themselves. And the lamps turning. And the steps of the doctor very fast, very fast.

"She can't labor any more, at six months nature does not help. She should have another injection."

I felt the needle thrust. The lamps were still. The ice and the blue that was all around came into my veins. My heart beat wildly. The nurses talked: "Now that baby of Mrs. L. last week, who would have thought she was too small, a big woman like that, a big woman like that, a big woman like that. . . ." The words kept turning, as on a disk. They talked, they talked, they talked. . . .

Please hold my legs! Please hold my legs! Please hold my legs! PLEASE HOLD MY LEGS! I am ready again. By throwing my head back I can see the clock. I have been struggling four hours. It would be better to die. Why am I alive and struggling so desperately? I could not remember why I should want to live. I could not remember any-thing. Everything was blood and pain. I have to push. I have to push. That is a black fixed point in eternity. At the end of a long dark tun-nel. I have to push. A voice saying: "Push! Push! Push!" A knee on my stomach and the marble of my legs crushing me and the head so large and I have to push.

Am I pushing or dying? The light up there, the immense round blazing white light is drinking me. It drinks me slowly, inspires me into space. If I do not close my eyes it will drink all of me. I seep up-ward, in long icy threads, too light, and yet inside there is a fire too, the nerves are twisted, there is no rest from this long tunnel dragging me, or am I pushing myself out of the tunnel, or is the child being pushed out of me, or is the light drinking me? Am I dying? The ice in the veins, the cracking of the bones, this pushing in darkness, with a small shaft of light in the eyes like the edge of a knife, the feeling of a knife cutting the flesh, the flesh somewhere is tearing as if it were burned through by a flame, somewhere my flesh is tearing and the blood is spilling out. I am pushing in the darkness, in utter darkness. I am pushing until my eyes open and I see the doctor holding a long instrument which he swiftly thrusts into me and the pain makes me cry out. A long animal howl. That will make her push, he says to the nurse. But it does not. It paralyzes me with pain. He wants to do it again. I sit up with fury and I shout at him: "Don't you dare do that again, don't you dare!"

The heat of my anger warms me, all the ice and pain are melted in the fury. I have an instinct that what he has done is unnecessary, that he has done it because he is in a rage, because the hands on the clock keep turning, the dawn is coming and the child does not come out, and I am losing strength and the injection does not produce the spasm.

I look at the doctor pacing up and down, or bending to look at the head which is barely showing. He looks baffled, as before a savage mystery, baffled by this struggle. He wants to interfere with his instruments, while I struggle with nature, with myself, with my child and with the meaning I put into it all, with my desire to give and to hold, to keep and to lose, to live and to die. No instrument can help me. His eyes are furious. He would like to take a knife. He has to watch and wait.

I want to remember all the time why I should want to live. I am all pain and no memory. The lamp has ceased drinking me. I am too weary to move even towards the light, or to turn my head and look at the clock. Inside of my body there are fires, there are bruises, the flesh is in pain. The child is not a child, it is a demon strangling me. The demon lies inert at the door of the womb, blocking life, and I cannot rid myself of it.

The nurses begin to talk again. I say: let me alone. I put my two hands on my stomach and very softly, with the tips of my fingers I drum drum drum drum drum drum on my stomach in circles. Around, around, softly, with eyes open in great serenity. The doctor comes near with amazement on his face. The nurses are silent. Drum drum drum drum drum drum in soft circles, soft quiet circles. Like a savage. The mystery. Eyes open, nerves begin to shiver, . . . a mysterious agitation. I hear the ticking of the clock . . . inexorably, separately. The little nerves awake, stir. But my hands are so weary, so weary, they will fall off. The womb is stirring and dilating. Drum

drum drum drum drum. I am ready! The nurse presses her knee on my stomach. There is blood in my eyes. A tunnel. I push into this tunnel, I bite my lips and push. There is a fire and flesh ripping and no air. Out of the tunnel! All my blood is spilling out. Push! Push! Push! It is coming! It is coming! It is coming! I feel the slipperiness, the sudden deliverance, the weight is gone. Darkness. I hear voices. I open my eyes. I hear them saying: "It was a little girl. Better not show it to her." All my strength returns. I sit up. The doctor shouts: "Don't sit up!"

"Show me the child!"

"Don't show it," says the nurse, "it will be bad for her." The nurses try to make me lie down. My heart is beating so loud I can hardly hear myself repeating: "Show it to me." The doctor holds it up. It looks dark and small, like a diminutive man. But it is a little girl. It has long eyelashes on its closed eyes, it is perfectly made, and all glistening with the waters of the womb.

Printed in the USA
CPSIA information can be obtained
at www.ICGtesting.com
LVHW020131071123
762936LV00005B/6